JanIus: Enter the King
Book 2
D.L. Hannah

Contents

Dedication   IV

1. Chapter 1   1

2. Chapter 2   20

3. Chapter 3   40

4. Chapter 4   60

5. Chapter 5   81

6. Chapter 6   102

7. Chapter 7   123

8. Chapter 8   143

9. Chapter 9   164

10. Chapter 10   188

11. Epilogue   205

Join my VIP list   210

Author Bio   211

Also by D.L. Hannah   212

Isis, I think we have another hit on our hands!

Chapter 1

King Belial stood barefoot in the water, staring at the figure floating toward him.

Sergeant Andon ran at full speed, stopping just at the bank's edge.

"Your Highness, our surveillance team found him. I'll call for the troops to transfer him to the worship chamber."

He stopped short at King Belial's raised hand.

"How long has he been here?"

The king's voice had barely raised above a whisper, but Sergeant Andon shivered under the sun's warm rays.

"Since last night, Your Majesty. We didn't want to bring the body ashore until you returned."

King Belial's eye took in every detail of what was left of his father. His scalp had been shaved clean.

"Why would they cut off his hair?" asked Sergeant Andon.

"She didn't kill him to take Platz because she didn't know if he was still the king or if he'd transferred the throne to me. That tells me he didn't tell her I'm still alive."

Removing an Azgote from his holster, he aimed it at the corpse's head and fired. The brain slid from the separated skull.

Sergeant Andon stared in horror when the king reached down and grabbed it before it reached the gentle waves.

He carefully turned the damaged mass around in his hand, scrutinizing the tiny wires and fixtures mapped around it. Sighing, he tossed it toward the body. It made a squishing sound when it hit the corpse's chest.

"She tried to turn my father into one of her mindless monsters, but it didn't work. When he didn't betray me, she ended him."

Rotating his shoulders in rapid succession, he said, "Oh, my little Queen Revari. When will you learn not to underestimate me?"

Eyeing the beginning stages of decomposition, he said, "Take the body to the incinerator."

"But, Your Majesty! Don't you want to give the former king a proper DeathCeremony?"

King Belial squinted into the sun. "My father died shortly after he entered Revani. I think he was saying goodbye when we had supper the other night. There's no need to drag any of this out."

Incensed by the bruising around the corpse's knuckles, he sloshed out of the water, and headed toward the palace. "Get it done, Andon."

Sergeant Andon saluted him. "Yes, My King!"

As he stared at King Belial's retreating form, he wondered if Queen Revari knew what kind of hell she'd just unleashed.

F awn looked at Justin as if he needed to check into the nearest wellness chamber.

"I have no idea what you're talking about, Dr. Ascencio. Until four years ago, I'd never stepped foot off JanIus. The only places I've been are Platirius and Revani to complete my studies. I've never been to Earth."

She twisted her wrist out of his grasp. "I think you've mistaken me for another Being."

Justin shook his head. "It was you. You might say I'm crazy, but you can't say I'm blind. You were dressed in Revaltian armor, and your fighting style was theirs. I saw you with my own eyes, Dr. Azini. Why don't you fess up and tell me what you want with me?"

Fawn blinked. "I don't want you. That might hurt your ego, but it's the truth."

"I'm not buying it. Something tells me if I go to Revani for answers, I won't know any more than I do now."

Fawn's irritated expression softened. "I heard you were a patient for a short while. Dr. Corning said you were seeing things that weren't there?"

Justin's lips thinned. "There's nothing wrong with my mind, so don't patronize me. I don't remember everything that caused me to pass out, but I'm definitely not crazy!"

She didn't look convinced.

"I just want to know why you saved me. I don't want to be at odds with you. Just tell me."

She took a step away from him. "I can't tell you what I don't know. It's clear you've been through something, and for the sake of argument, let's say a WomanForm brought you here. It wasn't me. I have no reason to lie to you."

"Then I guess we're at a standstill," said Justin.

She shook her head slowly as if he were three summers.

"No. You're standing all by yourself on this one. Now, if you don't mind, I have a million things to do to prepare for tomorrow. Please try to enjoy the rest of your evening."

Justin was about to say more when the door opened.

"Hey," said Gallium. "I came to check on you."

He looked from Fawn to Justin. "Am I interrupting something?"

"No," said Fawn. "We're finished here. It's nice to see you again, Gallium."

"You too, Dr. Azini," said Gallium.

"Well," said Gallium as Fawn made a quick exit. "How are you two getting along?"

Justin watched her walk away and sighed.

"We're not. She's the WomanForm who brought me here, but instead of admitting it, she tried to gaslight me into thinking I'm crazy. I'm not. I saw her, Gallium. She came to Earth and saved me from getting carted off to a lab."

Gallium frowned. "Fawn has been my student for two years. She doesn't seem like a liar."

"What army was she assigned to after graduation?"

Gallium's brow furrowed. "The Revaltians. Why?"

Justin rapped his knuckles on the desk. "I knew it! I knew she was lying to me!"

Gallium shifted a small box he was holding and raised a hand.

"Now hold on. Just because she's a Revaltian, that doesn't mean she went to Earth."

Justin opened a drawer and removed a small, pliable ball. "So, I didn't see her? I imagined everything?"

"Maybe the WomanForm you saw resembled Fawn, but wasn't her. I don't think you're crazy, but it's possible you're wrong on this one. She's been under strict supervision for years. Who would send her for you?"

Justin stared at him, rapidly squeezing the ball.

"Oh, come on. Queen Revari could've sent me or Legend if she wanted to bring you back. We have seniority over Fawn and know Earth like the backs of our hands. It doesn't make sense for her to use Fawn to bring you here."

Justin sat down in his chair and sighed. He didn't want to admit it, but Gallium's words made sense.

"So why am I here?" asked Justin.

Gallium shrugged. "I don't know, but it's probably not good for you to stay in Space. Look at what's happened in the short time you've been here. If you don't want to return to the United States, you can settle down in another spot."

"It sounds like you don't want me here."

Gallium took a seat across from him. "That's not it. There's nothing I want more than to see you and Queen Revari make up for lost time. But you've never dealt with King Dubian or his father. They ruled Platirius for more years than even I can count. The power they held was immeasurable and...unchallenged."

He leaned in closer to Justin. "As long as you're here, they'll never let up on you. You're the last male of the Amorous royal line. They want you on the throne, and they'll destroy anything in their path to get it—even you."

Justin wiped a hand over his eyes. He felt drained—spiritually and mentally.

"Here," said Gallium, pushing the fancy decorated box across to him. "A little get well present."

Uncrossing his legs, Justin set the ball aside, expertly removing the iridescent paper.

Gallium squinted. "I don't think I've ever seen a box opened with so much care."

"I don't like ruining nice things," said Justin.

He gently pushed the paper aside and opened the box. Frowning, he reached inside and lifted a pair of orange baby booties.

"Uh, Gallium. I haven't impregnated anyone."

Gallium shook his head and laughed. "Too much information."

Examining the booties more closely, he said, "These look ancient but brand new."

Gallium held a smile and nodded toward the box. "There's more. Keep going."

The next item was a beautiful snow globe. Peering at it closely, he observed a family. The mother held up a laughing infant, while the father stood behind her with his hands on her shoulders. Both were smiling at the baby.

Gallium swept a finger under and up. "Push the button underneath."

Justin flipped over the globe and pressed a small button. Snow began falling around the family as they danced in a circle. Raising the globe closer to his face, Justin sucked in a breath. He recognized the family—it was his.

I'm the baby!

Carefully focusing on the father, he whispered, "He looks just like me. And this is Mama."

His attention shifted to the booties again. "Are these mine?"

"Yep," said Gallium proudly. "After King Dubian had your mother locked away, Legend and I went to Cuba and packed everything she and her husband bought the last time they were together. She's kept them all this time."

His cloudy eyes found Gallium's. "Who made the globe?"

Gallium sat back with a satisfied grin. "I did."

"You knew my father?"

"No, but Queen Revari has dozens of paintings of him throughout the palace. She's a very talented artist. It took some time to make it, but I thought you'd appreciate a nice gift."

Justin wiped away a lone tear. "This is...I don't know what to say, Gallium. Thank you."

"It's what could have been," said Gallium. "Sometimes we want to rewrite the past, but it only ends up hurting us more."

As Justin stared at the dancing family, Gallium said, "You're not my grandson, but you could've been had Queen Dellah married me instead of King Dubian. I imagine Coldarius would still be here, and everyone's lives would've been better."

He frowned. "But that's not what happened. All we can do is cherish what we have now and try to forget the wrongs done to us. If we let it, the past can reach out from the grave and destroy the future."

The snow globe wobbled a bit in Justin's trembling hands.

"I don't want to see you get hurt," said Gallium. "It doesn't matter if you're on JanIus or Revani, Platirius's ghosts are still powerful. They'll never let you rest."

Justin sniffed. "Did Queen Revari send you here to tell me to go?"

"No. She doesn't know I'm here. I came because I wanted to."

Gallium folded his hands on the desk. "You're nothing like King Dubian. You remind me of King Carlomon—kind and ready to help anyone in need. But even kind Beings can be tempted to become evil. I watched your need for revenge drive Queen Vivant deeper into insanity."

He bowed his head. "At the time, I didn't stop you because I was angry with her for not protecting your mother. As time went on, I realized that wasn't her job—it was mine. I promised Queen Dellah I'd protect both of her daughters, but I failed."

Justin gently set the snow globe on the desk. The dancing figures swayed to the soft, melancholy tune flowing in the air.

"I suspect King Dubian or King Anemi is after you."

A sharp pain flashed through Justin's skull. Grunting, he leaned forward, clutching the top of his head. Gallium jumped up and rushed to him.

"Justin?"

"I'm alright. Wow, that came out of nowhere."

"No, I don't think it did," said Gallium. "I'm right on this one. One or both of the kings has come for you. They'll continue attacking you until you do as they say. That means taking down Queen Vivant for the throne."

Gallium placed a hand on his shoulder. "I understand the pain of losing a father, but I can't let you hurt her this time."

"I don't want to hurt anyone. Listen, I don't know why I was brought here, but I do know I followed someone who looked a lot like Fawn. I'm not interested in Platirius and—"

"You don't have to be," interrupted Gallium. "Platirius's spirits are interested in you. That's what matters. You're not safe here."

"I understand," said Justin. "But I can't leave until I know who wanted me and why."

Observing Gallium's worried expression, he said, "I appreciate you caring about me. You're the closest thing I have to a friend here. Believe me, no one is more weirded out by everything that's happened than I am, but I have to uncover the truth."

Gingerly touching the small, dancing family, he said, "There's a reason I returned to Space. Somehow, King Carlomon is right in the middle of it. I think he wants me to help him. I couldn't live with myself if I didn't."

Gallium patted his shoulder and sat down again. "What do you mean?"

Justin leaned forward in anticipation. "Enter the king. What does it mean?"

Gallium's lips formed an O. "I honestly don't know. There's about a thousand realms in the galaxy and all are run by kings except Platirius and Revani. Where did you hear it?"

"King Carlomon said it to me in my dream. He was sitting in a small room with a one-way window."

"You were inside his palace!" exclaimed Gallium. "I built that room for him. He used it for painting and sculpting figures."

Justin paused. Not wanting to bring up painful memories for Gallium, he wondered if he should confide in him about the dreams.

Gallium read his mind. "Tell me. I'm not a ChildForm. Don't hold anything back."

"It's where he died," said Justin. "I think someone put him in that room and slit his wrist. Blood was everywhere. He wore a small blue stone on a chain that the killer stole. I saw a shadow, but couldn't see his face. He cut me with a knife that had two lions on it and the initials DA."

"Dubian Amorous," said Gallium. He swore, slapping his hands hard on his thighs. "I knew he killed him, but I didn't know how! What else did you see?"

"King Carlomon told me to find the stone. What does it represent?"

"It's the CarogueStone. Coldarius and King Carlomon's lifeforces were tied to it. If he'd died under normal circumstances, Queen Opal would've claimed it. Every ruler who sits on a throne is assigned a LifeStone. It's inherited through the generations. King Dubian must have stolen it when he murdered him. That means..."

"It might still be on Platirius," finished Justin.

"Even if it is, you can't go there. If the kings' spirits are powerful enough to get to you here, they'll eat you alive on Platirius."

"It's only one," said Justin. "He said his name was...King Anemi."

"He's the worst of them. He's much more powerful than his sons."

Gallium stretched out his legs, thinking. "Anemi was a powerful sorcerer before he became king. The black magic he wielded will never die—it's a part of Platirius."

He looked up at Justin. "If you go there searching for the CarogueStone, you may not get out of there whole."

"Well, I doubt Queen Vivant will hand it over to me with a smile. Coldarius's essence is a part of Platirius. She'll want to keep it intact."

Justin cupped his chin in his hand. "So, King Dubian murdered King Carlomon and absorbed Coldarius into Platirius. What if King Carlomon wants me to undo what he did? What would happen if Platirius and Coldarius were separated again?"

Gallium shook his head slowly, then sighed. "I don't know. It's never been done before. And everyone is dead. It's not as if Coldarius would be a whole planet again. What would you accomplish by reversing the absorption?"

"I don't know," Justin admitted. "But I think that's exactly what he wants me to do. I have to get my hands on that CarogueStone, Gallium. Then...then my job will be done and I can return to Earth. You didn't see him. His eyes were so sad. There's no way his soul is at peace."

"That's not something I like hearing. It's been comforting to think he and Queen Dellah are resting peacefully."

Gallium ran his hands through his shoulder-length hair. "Queen Vivant loved her grandfather. If she has the CarogueStone, she won't let him go just like that. You're risking a lot by going to see her."

"I know, but I can't afford to think about myself. He's reached out to me for help. I can't let him down."

Gallium sighed. "I hope things go the way you want them to."

Justin smiled sadly. "I hope so too. If Queen Vivant won't help me..."

"She won't," said Gallium sagely.

"Then I'll just have to find a way. I have no clue why the female soldier brought me here, but JanIus is wrapped up in the mystery too. King Leighton said it was a new planet. Do you know how it was founded?"

"King Leighton's great-grandfather took the throne a couple of years after Coldarius froze. I heard what was left of our Coldarian army settled on it after leaving Platirius, but I never followed up on it. I don't know anything about JanIus's royal family. They've kept a low profile."

"Well, I know you're against me going to Platirius, but it's the only way I'll find answers."

"I don't want to see you get hurt, is all," said Gallium.

"Why? Because of Mom?"

Gallium shook his head. "That's part of it. The main thing is, I knew all of the Amorous kings. Especially King Dubian. He was my rival."

Gallium frowned, reliving the toxic memories.

"King Tylo literally hid behind a mask so no one from Old Platirius would recognize him when he took over Pletz. I remember how deceptive they were. They want their power back and will do anything to get it. I don't want to see you get caught up in the crossfire. Let me go with you if you need to go to Platirius. If anything happens, I'll be there to help. "

The dancing family stilled when Justin turned off the music. "Sounds like a plan. Thank you for looking out for me."

"No problem. When are you planning to go?"

"How about tonight?"

Gallium nodded. "Alright. The sooner we get it over with, the better off we'll all be."

Fawn finished checking the inventory and exited the main supply closet. All the supplies were up to date and fully stocked. She'd inspected the medical chamber from top to bottom.

Nothing was out of place. Dr. Ascencio had ensured everything from the state-of-the-art medical equipment and furnishings to the highly polished floors was in top condition. She hadn't expected that.

Suspecting the never-ending duties might've overwhelmed him, she'd been prepared to fire him and send him on his way. Except King Leighton had appointed him. That meant he wouldn't be going anywhere unless the king ordered it.

Expelling a frustrated breath, she reflected on the strange conversation. Why would he think she'd gone to Earth? She'd never seen it, nor did she have any desire to.

There was no reason for her to want him on JanIus either. He was a MaleForm. An arrogant one at that. And extremely handsome. Fawn suspected he was aware of the latter.

Well, none of the doctor's charms would sway her. Her father was finally gone forever. The largest medical chamber on JanIus now belonged to her. She wasn't about to share any authoritative duties with a stranger.

Or any Being for that matter. She assumed the MaleForm patients wouldn't make taking over the practice easy for her, but she was ready for them too. Either they would get on board with her vision, or they could travel elsewhere to receive medical care. It was her time now.

It was late before she finally turned the key in the door. She wanted a hot bath and a good night's rest. Tomorrow would be her first day as the Chief ParaNurture Physician. She'd sent a transmission to all the staff calling for a meeting the next morning.

She wanted to ensure everyone that the practice was in good hands. Thanks to both of the queens' generosity, she had a fully functioning medical staff that could handle any emergency.

"Fawn? Is that you?" asked Musha.

Fawn braced herself. She hadn't seen her mother since the graduation ceremony. She wasn't looking forward to discussing her father's death.

Musha entered the dining chamber, wringing her hands. "I haven't heard from your father. Did he return from Revani with you?"

"No, Mother. Why would he when he came with you?"

"But Queen Revari had him stay for a meeting. He's never been this late coming home before."

Fawn raised an eyebrow. "Maybe something caught his attention."

Musha shook her head furiously. "No. The new ParaNurture physician begins tomorrow. He told me he wanted to find out who it was so that he could train him personally."

Fawn's crooked smile held no warmth. "It's not a male, Mother. It's a female. The new ParaNurture physician is me."

Musha's eyes widened. "Fawn, there's no way your father will let you work in his practice. You know that!"

"I don't think he has much say in anything now, Mother. If you'll excuse me, I'm going to bed. I have a lot to do tomorrow."

"Aren't you the least bit worried about him?" cried Musha.

Fawn turned and stared at her mother. After everything he'd done to them, she couldn't understand how her mother still loved him.

"I would say what I think, but I doubt you'd want to hear it. If you want to stay up and wait for him, that's fine. I'm going to bed. Good night, Mother."

As she ascended the stairs, Musha called up to her. "Queen Revari spent all that time and funding preparing you for a career you'll never have! She wasted everyone's time, including yours. Freddi is still waiting. Why don't you call him and tell him you were wrong?"

She tentatively stepped back as her daughter stood at the top of the stairs, staring at her with a coldness she'd never seen before.

"Wrong? The only one who's ever been wrong in this house is the MaleForm you married! Don't think I'm stupid enough to follow in your footsteps. Not only am I a doctor, I'm a warrior.

I don't need a MaleForm for funding or protection, Mother. That's something you'll never be able to say with a straight face."

She turned and left Musha standing there, wondering what had happened to her sweet and obedient daughter.

G eneral Lyric entered and bowed before Queen Vivant. "My Queen, someone is here to see you."

Queen Vivant looked up from entering data into her personal TranScreen. "Who is it, Lyric?"

General Lyric bit her lip. "It's Prince Justin. He says it's imperative that he speaks with you."

The queen's hands stilled. She looked from Lyric to the closed door of her meeting chamber. Deja vu flooded her as she reflected on the last time Queen Revari had been on the other side of her desk.

Nodding at the general, she said, "Send him in."

"Do you need me to stay?"

"No. I doubt he's here to cause trouble. He probably thinks I'll transmit our mother's photos to him. Clearly, he's come to hear in person what I've already stated."

"Yes, My Queen."

The door opened when she scanned her hand across the TeleShield, revealing the prince standing patiently on the other side.

"Don't say anything to upset her," she whispered to him.

Noting every detail of her lovely face, he said, "I wouldn't dream of it, General. Are you free for dinner tonight?"

She paused, staring up at him in shock. "You never quit, do you?"

"Is there a reason I should? I hear Platirius has opened its doors to MaleForms. Have you fallen in love since I've been gone?"

He hid a smile at her indignant frown. "Of course not. Falling in love isn't for me!"

"Don't bet the farm, General," he teased.

Her puzzled expression almost made him laugh. "The what?"

"I take it you don't watch a lot of Human shows in Space."

"I don't have time for frivolous things."

"Ah yes, you still don't know what fun is." He lowered his tone. "Or kissing."

Startled, her violet-gray eyes flew to his green ones.

"I'll let you get back to your strenuous duties then," he whispered.

She saluted him sharply, then marched off.

What a WomanForm! he thought.

His amused expression fizzled when he looked into the cool, silver eyes of his aunt.

"Prince Justin? You're full of surprises, aren't you? I thought we had an understanding I'm not giving you my mother's photos."

He strode in and took a seat across from her. "I'm not here about the photos."

Her eyebrow quirked. "No?"

He shook his head. "Nope. I'm more interested in what you can tell me about King Carlomon."

Chapter 2

Her expression was unreadable. He now understood why Gallium had dubbed her the "Ice Queen." Unlike Queen Revari, she didn't fly off the handle on a whim, nor did she readily say what was on her mind.

While his mother's eyes sparkled with vivid emotion—elation, anger, or annoyance—Queen Vivant's didn't. Everything about her was carefully measured.

Calculated, he thought.

Under her icy scrutiny, he felt like a specimen in a research chamber. A slight shiver went up his spine.

"What do you want to know about my grandfather?"

Justin crossed his foot over his knee. "He visits my dreams."

Her face remained as still as stone.

Clearing his throat, Justin said, "I think he wants me to help him. Did you know he was murdered?"

She blinked once. Slowly. He couldn't tell if it was an affirmation or a denial. Several beats of silence passed between them. When he realized she wasn't going to say anything, he kept going.

"There was a small room in the palace he painted in. The killer took him there and slit his wrist. He bled to death in that room. And there's more. He showed me a small blue stone, about the size of a dime, on a chain around his neck. It looked like a topaz. He told me the killer took it and..."

He stared into her eyes. "He told me he was murdered."

Her gaze, never wavering from his, was as ominous and forbidden as a black hole in Space. Finally, she closed her eyes, expelling a breath before opening them again. "It's no secret my father murdered my grandfather. The only way to take a planet is to kill its ruler. I lived in my grandfather's palace. Ate with him at his table. Sat with him while he read stories to me before bedtime. I often played in the room you speak of. Yet, here you sit telling me he's visited you and not me? Why would he come to you, a stranger?"

She leaned back in the chair and frowned. "Do you believe you're more special to him than I?"

"I don't think I'm better than anyone, Queen Vivant. I'm merely here to get answers. If you don't believe me, then how do I know what his art room looked like when I've never been on Coldarius?"

"I never said you were lying. I asked why you think you're above an Amorous queen. Is it because you're half MaleForm?"

He let out a harsh laugh. "What does that have to do with anything?"

"All MaleForms think they're better than WomenForms. Even half ones, it seems."

Her half smile was absent of warmth. "I remember the CarogueStone. He was wearing it on the night we had supper as a family for the last time. He never took it off. No ruler does."

She tapped a small diamond secured around a platinum chain on her neck. "This belonged to King Anemi, then my father, and now it's mine."

Justin nodded at the stone. "You inherited it when Platirius split? What did my mother get?"

"Rubarius. And everything that came with it. Before hearing this, I assumed the CarogueStone was destroyed with King Carlomon." She met his eyes. "I don't know where it is now. And if I had it, I wouldn't give it to you. I wouldn't give it to any Being—it's that precious to our family."

"Am I not a part of your family?" asked Justin.

"Mmmm... Yes, but a MaleForm. Do you really think I'd hand that kind of power over to you? You have much to learn about our way of life. I don't mind informing you no MaleForm descendant will ever lead Platirius."

"I don't want Platirius. My motivation is to help King Carlomon."

"I'm not convinced he needs your assistance," she said coldly. "He died when I was a ChildForm. His heart was better and purer than any Being I've ever met. I'm certain he ascended to The One's realm. Yet, you'd like me to believe his soul wanders about the galaxy, needing you to set him free? That's quite a story."

He'd been careful not to say anything to bring up painful memories for Gallium, but he hadn't considered that confiding in her would shatter her world too.

He realized that while Queen Revari was an explosive reactor, Queen Vivant had kept a tight lid on her trauma since childhood.

May God help us all if she ever explodes.

For the first time, he felt remorse for what he'd done to her.

"I apologize for leading you to believe you were crazy. It was a terrible thing to do."

"You were under the influence of Revari's BrainStaff, correct?"

"Yes, but that's no excuse."

She folded her hands and gently placed them atop the desk. "Do you think you would've done it if there were no BrainStaff?"

He blinked once. "Well...no. I admit I was angry when I heard you played a role in my father's death, but I don't have it in me to hurt anyone. I'd rather let karma take care of things."

"Karma?" she echoed. "What's that?"

"The universe's way of serving justice."

She shook her head dismissively. "I've never heard of that."

He smiled halfheartedly. "I think it's only something Humans believe in."

She tapped a single finger on the desk. Once. "I can believe it. Would you like something to drink? I don't indulge in spirits like my sister, but I have a variety of selections here."

She nodded toward a small room with an enormous ice box, a sanitizing station, and a round dining table that made him sit up and take notice.

"May I take a closer look at your table?"

She looked puzzled but said, "Of course."

Swallowing hard, Justin got up and approached the table. It looked exactly as it did in his dreams. Peering at it closely, he saw tiny engraved initials on the side of the tabletop. *VEA. RAA. DCA. KCC. OCA.* Queen Vivant stood next to him, looking down at the table.

"Vivant Elizabeth Amorous. Revari Ava Amorous. Della Carogue-Amorous. Kent Carlomon Carogue. Opal Carogue-Amorous. I carved these the first night I was in Grandfather Carlomon's palace. I remember our first supper together."

She smiled fondly at the carvings, tracing them with the tip of her manicured, silver nail. "I thought if I wrote our names on this table, we'd never be apart."

Her smile slowly vanished. "How silly of me," she whispered.

"So this table was in King Carlomon's palace?"

She nodded. "He had it shipped here when Aunt Opal married my father. He said he hoped it would make me feel less lonely."

She looked around the room. "This used to be Aunt Opal's sitting room. After she died, Revari and I would play in here and retrace the initials when we were sad—which was often. Father was always making someone angry. We weren't well liked by the other ChildForms, but they knew better than to let us know it." Her pretty features darkened. "Father would've punished them."

Suddenly, she turned to him. "Why don't you stay for supper? You haven't met my daughters yet—your cousins. It would be nice to sit down and break bread as a family."

"I...oh...well, I didn't come alone."

"Oh? Did Revari come with you?"

"No. Gallium is here too."

She winced. "Gallium? Why did you bring him?"

"He says the old kings want to possess my soul. He knew your father well, so he says he can protect me from them."

"Gallium and my father were enemies until the day he died, but my mother loved him very much. I did too...once."

"What happened between the two of you?"

"He turned on me for Revari."

"That's not true," said a deep voice.

They turned and saw Gallium standing in the middle of her meeting chamber.

"I never turned on you. I just couldn't stomach you not protecting your sister when you should've."

"That was your job," she shot back. "It was you who sat at my mother's deathbed and promised her you'd protect her, not me. I was a ChildForm too. Who was I to go up against a king as powerful as Father?"

Gallium inclined his head. "Touche, Queen Vivant."

"You certainly came through for Revari. But you left me standing on the sidelines."

"King Dubian and General Kron gave you the sun and moon," he fired back. "All you had to do was wake up and ask. What did Revari get? Scorn. Betrayal."

"On my day of judgement, it will be The One on the throne before me, not you, Gallium. If you've come here to remind me of my sins, you may leave."

"I just came to make sure no harm would come to Prince Justin."

She laughed bitterly. "Revari. Justin. Legend. You protect everyone in the galaxy except me. I wonder what you'll say to my mother when you see her again."

"It'll be between she and I," said Gallium.

She'd hit a nerve. Queen Dellah was his Achilles' heel, but the queen wasn't wrong—he hadn't protected her, and not only for turning her back on Revari. He blamed her father and husband for losing Coldarius.

Since they weren't around, he'd secretly held it against her. That surprised him. He hadn't realized he was capable of holding a grudge until she reminded him that's precisely what he'd done.

"Well, I guess I'm not invited to supper. Prince Justin, I'll be waiting by the craft."

When he turned to go, she said, "No. Please stay. We have plenty. My mother would never forgive me if I excluded you."

Gallium's smile was sad. "Her daughters could never make her angry. I wish I could say that was true for you and Queen Revari."

"It'll work itself out in the end," she said.

She went to her desk and cleared it off. She couldn't abide a mess. "Come. Meet my daughters. General Lyric and Captain TamRi will be joining us too."

She cocked her head toward Gallium. "You remember General Lyric, don't you?"

"Yes. She's General Iham's daughter."

She froze, a small adding machine still in her hand. "I haven't heard that name in ages. Who was her mother?"

"Lady Alarah," said Gallium. "She's imprisoned in the Flames of Justice."

She put the adding machine in the drawer and closed it firmly. "What? Why? How did she get there?"

"She betrayed Coldarius. She told King Dubian how to break in and steal you, your sister, and your aunt."

Queen Vivant and Prince Justin's mouth dropped.

"How do you know this?" asked Queen Vivant.

"I was outside Platirius's gates with General Iham when your father married your aunt. He had her beaten in front of everyone and tossed into the Flames after they took their vows."

"I knew Father abused women, but I never thought Lyric's mother was one of them! Does she know?"

"No. And I'll never tell her. Her father was the epitome of honorable, but her mother was a cold, spiteful WomanForm. She deserved what she got."

"I have the power to set her free. She's Lyric's mother, and Coldarius is gone now. What purpose would it serve to keep her there?"

"She sold Lyric for power. King Dubian lied to her, promising he'd make her queen if she helped him. She didn't care about Lyric then, and she won't the minute she steps foot out of the Flames. It's your call, Your Highness, but I think it's best for everyone if she continues burning."

Justin looked from Gallium to the queen. "He's right. My birth parents didn't raise me, but sometimes it's best if the toxic one stays gone. I don't want Lyric to get hurt."

Queen Vivant chewed on her bottom lip. "Neither do I. I had no idea she was imprisoned here. Very well. Her punishment will stand. For Lyric's sake."

"Please never tell her," said Gallium. "I don't think she could handle hearing the truth about her mother."

"But Lyric has always wanted to know where she came from. She believes she was abandoned by both of her parents."

"That's a lie. General Iham tried to get her back when he returned to Platirius to work under Queen Opal. But she wouldn't order the adoptive family to return her to him. He tried to see her every day, but they wouldn't allow it. I know. I was there. He died wondering if she knew how much he loved her."

Gallium searched inside his pocket and took out a silver fish on a delicate platinum chain. Its eyes were blue sapphires. "Here, give this to her. He made it for her. But never tell her where it came from."

"You were her father's friend. Shouldn't you give it to her?"

"General Lyric asks more questions than even this one." He hooked a thumb in Justin's direction. "If it comes from me, she won't stop until she learns the truth. I don't mind telling her about her father, but I don't want her to know the role her mother played in Coldarius's demise. Billions of Beings were murdered, including our king. No ChildForm should ever bear the burden of their parents' choices."

Queen Vivant nodded. "I agree. Let us go to supper."

Justin expected everyone to be stiff and formal. To his surprise, they had laughed and joked together as if they'd known each other forever. He found Princess Teenah and Tyre to be quite jovial. Princess Tarah, however, was more reserved.

He noted she was polite, yet sensed she didn't trust him. He didn't blame her. He wouldn't trust anyone who had hurt his mother either. An instant connection formed between Gallium and Captain TamRi. They talked quietly together as Princess Teenah did a hilarious impression of General Legend. She nearly fainted when Gallium smiled.

Queen Vivant signaled for the first course: oyster stew, cream of mushroom soup, and spinach salad with bacon and blue cheese.

The dining staff served the main course of risotto with mushrooms and caramelized onions, parsnip puree with olive oil, crab cakes, scallops seared in butter, baked trout, shrimp scampi, and crab ravioli in a creamy, garlicky sauce. Strong, finely brewed coffee, tea, crème brulee, lemon and raspberry pavlovas, and orange curd tarts complemented the meal.

Between the shrimp scampi and the ravioli, Justin thought he would burst. The different shapes and textures of the food never ceased to fascinate him. He found all of it delicious. He was careful to suppress murmurs of pleasure—at the food and at the sight of General Lyric.

She'd traded her usual military uniform for a simple dress made of the softest powder blue silk he'd ever wanted to touch.

Her sandy brown hair was a stylish pixie cut that accentuated her high cheekbones, full lips, and almond-shaped, violet-gray eyes. He wanted to kiss the cute mole in the middle of her right cheek and another smaller one just above her brow.

Gallium recognized the silver heart earrings and necklace she wore. General Iham had purchased them for Lady Alarah shortly after they married. The general wore clear, sleek gloss on her lips and just a touch of mascara and liner on her eyes. He shot a sly look at the queen, who was taking careful note of her nephew and general.

Looks as if someone might be playing matchmaker, thought Gallium.

Prince Justin struggled not to ogle her. He'd never seen her in anything other than her military gear and the dress didn't hide an ounce of her enticing form. She wasn't as well-endowed as General Legend, nor did she need to be in his eyes.

He found the size of her breasts just right—not too large or too small. The scent of her subtle, flowery perfume was driving him over the edge. He scooted his chair closer to the table to hide his rising member, and added a pavlova to his plate.

Gallium wiped his mouth and inclined his head toward the courtyard at Queen Vivant. She noted the subtle cue. He wanted to discuss something in private with her.

"Please continue enjoying dessert. I'll return shortly. Gallium?"

The rose in unison. "After you, Your Highness."

Staring straight ahead at an enormous statue of Queen Dellah perched atop the massive mausoleum, she said, "I'm glad you came with Prince Justin, Gallium. We haven't had a chance to talk since the night we lost Coldarius. How have you been?"

He, too, looked up at the impressive image of the queen, immortally encased in pure diamond. It had stood the test of time. He ought to know. He had built it.

"I'm well, Queen Vivant. As I said, I came to make sure nothing happened to Prince Justin."

"We must keep Queen Revari happy, yes?"

"You have no reason to be angry with your sister. You've wronged her many times over."

"Blunt and to the point as always, aren't you? Why did you want to speak to me alone?"

"King Dubian destroyed Coldarius but it could've been prevented."

She turned and stared at him. "How?"

"Your husband. General Kron knew your father wanted to annihilate Coldarius."

She waved her hand at him. "I don't believe that for one second. Lucian knew it was my mother's birth home. He'd never do anything to hurt me."

"He knew, Queen Vivant. He only confessed because Queen Opal threatened to ship him into the sun. He told her everything."

"You've always hated Lucian. Why should I believe you?"

He chuckled. "Do you think he had any love for me?"

The memory she'd found when she scanned Dora's brain came flooding back. "What really happened to my husband?" she asked suddenly.

If the question caught him off guard, he didn't show it.

"I have no idea what you're talking about."

She moved closer to him, her beautiful eyes glowing a strange blue under the low lights.

"Oh, I think you do. You're my sister's right hand. She doesn't make a move without you knowing about it. You and that General Legend." Her chilly smile widened. "I hear she's my father's bastard. How inappropriate of him."

Gallium held his emotions in check. After all this time, something had piqued her interest in her husband's death. He knew both daughters were like their mother...and their father. Queen Vivant was looking for blood, but if she thought she'd spill his or Legend's, he had news for her.

"I told you, I don't know. I heard he'd been killed in battle—same as everyone else. I don't know why you're looking into this now."

"A body was never found," she said. "Now I'm learning there was a reason for that—there was no battle on Saturn. Queen Marietta informed me of this. She and his father were expecting us that day, but we didn't go."

Visibly upset, she began pacing back and forth, a habit she'd inherited from her Aunt Opal. "After all these years, his personal pilot contacted me, informing me he had to tell me something, but he died before he had a chance. All of these things cannot be coincidences."

Gallium glanced up at the statue again. "Whether they are or they aren't, it has nothing to do with me. Your husband had me beheaded."

"If that's true, then how are you alive?"

"Oh, come on! You're not the only one gifted with power."

"I'm aware, but if you were beheaded, there's no way you would've come back from that," she spat. "It's impossible."

He shook his head. "With Beings, it's impossible. Nothing is impossible for The One."

She moved closer to him. "So you, too, are a Guardian for The One? An immortal soldier in His army? Is that what you're telling me?"

"Me too? Who else is there?"

Her eyes shone with a new secret she wouldn't reveal.

"Do you remember the promise you made to my mother before she died?"

His lips thinned. "This again? I've never forgotten anything about Queen Dellah—especially our conversations. But I don't see what it has to do with you."

"It has everything to do with me." She cocked her head. "Your tongue says you haven't forgotten your promise, but your actions are quite another story. My mother told me you promised to keep my sister and I safe. But you only kept half of her promise."

"We're going in circles here. You had a husband and a father who catered to your every whim. There was no one you needed protection from. Queen Revari had no one to protect her—thanks to you. There's nothing wrong with my memory, but maybe you've forgotten all the pain you caused her?"

"I forget nothing. I still remember how kind you were to me at Mother's DeathCeremony. I'm just wondering why you stopped being my friend? I helped you in your moment of need."

"You mean when I lost my mind after your father destroyed my family and my planet?"

His lips curved slightly. "Thanks for the nap, but the memories have stayed with me all this time."

"I've never meant you any harm."

"Good, then I'll thank you to stay out of my mind. It's rude to read thoughts that don't belong to you, Your Highness."

"I can read your mind because I'm half-Coldarian and Queen Dellah's eldest daughter! You say my father gave me things as if that makes all of this alright! It doesn't. I emulated him by giving my daughters everything too."

She pointed at him. "But you know what? That's all I was left with when I thought they were dead—useless things I wanted to burn but couldn't because then I'd lose everything! I've suffered too, Gallium! Why do you refuse to admit it? You can't hold Revari close to your heart and cast me out as if I don't belong to my mother just as much as she does!"

She had him there. He bowed his head. "You're right. I failed Queen Dellah by not being there for you. But even you have to admit King Dubian and General Kron never allowed me to get as close to you as Queen Revari."

Her eyes filling with tears, she nodded. "Yes, that's true. Lucian thought you might seduce me."

Anger coursed through him. "I remember when you were an InfantForm. Do you know how sick that would've been had I even thought to do something so vile?"

She blinked back tears. "My father and husband were the only examples I had of how MaleForms conducted themselves. Lucian was my best friend. I had no reason not to trust him."

"He lied to you out of jealousy. I could never be in love with you any more than I could your sister."

A spark of merriment danced in her eyes. "Because you were in love with my mother."

He opened his mouth and closed it.

She took a step toward him. "You *were* in love with her, weren't you? You could've been our FatherForm. Do you ever wish you could go back and change things? Would you have told her how you felt about her?"

He sighed. "What's done is done. I've been in love with Legend for most of my life. I don't regret a minute I've spent with her—not even the bad times."

"You mean when she tossed you aside like a rotten potato for her career?"

He looked at her suspiciously. "How do you know that?"

"I was an observant ChildForm back then. I saw you tell her you had nothing left for her when she returned from Earth. I see things have sorted themselves out. She never needed your protection, but I did."

She turned to stare at the statue again. "With Mother gone, his madness permeated every corner of every chamber of this palace. He interfered in my marriage more times than I can count."

"I'm sorry about what the king did to you, but I'll never feel sorry for General Kron. And this is why," he said, holding up his palm.

She turned her palm upward to his. "What's this?"

"I downloaded it from the surveillance chamber before King Dubian had all of the surveillance staff killed. It's General Kron's confession to being an accessory to King Dubian murdering everyone on Coldarius. If he were alive today, I wouldn't stop until he was brought in front of a justice council or I'd take his head myself. You need proof your husband would lie to you? There it is."

He sighed. "I don't want to fight with you anymore. You've reminded me of my promise to your mother, and I own everything I didn't do for you. I'll make it up to you too. But you have to see the truth about Kron. Had he told someone—anyone, Coldarius might still be here."

She looked down at her palm. "I'll review the data. What happens between us now?"

"We'll get to know each other again. Slowly."

"I doubt your wife would like that."

His confident smile reminded her of the way things were. "Well, my wife doesn't own me."

"I'll never accept her as my father's daughter. Never."

"Then we finally agree on something, because I'll never accept your husband was a decent Being. Not ever. As long as you don't try to hurt Legend, I see no reason why we can't rebuild our friendship."

"I have no interest in her. Shall we return? They're probably finished eating by now."

He bowed. "Lead the way, Your Highness."

"You bowed to us like that the last time we all had dinner together—you, Revari, Aunt Opal, and I. We had a good time before everything blew to hell."

He smiled inwardly at the bittersweet memory. "Yes, we did, Your Majesty."

She closed her hand into a tight fist. No matter how much she wanted to avoid it, she owed it to herself to know the truth about that fateful night. She and Gallium walked side by side through the palace doors, leaving the fierce pride in Queen Dellah's face shining in the moon's light.

"They're not here, Mother. They left a short while ago," said Princess Teenah.

The queen's eyebrow rose. "What do you mean, they left?"

Princess Teenah shrugged. "They took a TravelCraft back to JanIus. General Lyric said it's her night off and Prince Justin said

Gallium would take Aunt Reve's craft back to Revani after you two finished talking."

The princess was nearly bursting with excitement.

"They looked so cute together!" she gushed.

Gallium shook his head in amusement. "I'd better get going. Thank you for having me for supper."

When he bowed to Princess Teenah, her eyes grew wider than WarCrafts.

"Don't even think about it, young WomanForm," whispered Queen Vivant.

"But, Mother, I'm twenty summers!" she groaned.

"He's old enough to be your grandfather, and he's married."

The light went out of the princess's face faster than a cloud covering the sun.

"Oh. He's married," she said glumly.

Queen Vivant laughed aloud. "So his age doesn't bother you, hm?"

"With a face and body like that? Never!"

"Princess Teenah!"

"Sorry, Mother! Goodbye, General Barrios!"

She waved and ran off, leaving Gallium to wonder where she got her bubbly personality.

Gallium bowed to Queen Vivant again. "Good night, Your Highness."

"Good night, General Barrios."

Chapter 3

The TravelCraft's engine's low humming was barely audible as Justin and Lyric rode quietly into the night.

"I love JanIus this time of night," said Justin. "It's the most beautiful thing I've ever seen."

She watched him mentally devour her. "Besides you, of course."

Blushing, she turned away, looking out into the night. "What's that sitting on the edge of the bank?" she asked, pointing across the large expanse of water.

"That small building? That cafe serves some of the best food I've ever eaten. I often have lunch there."

"Do you like working in the main medical chamber?"

"I love it! There's nothing better than helping Beings get well."

She turned to him. "Why did you come back? The last time you were in Space, you were so angry, I thought I'd never see you again."

He shrugged. "It's a long story. I honestly don't know why I'm here, but I intend to find out." He ran a finger down the base of her spine. "Are you admitting you wanted to see me?"

He cupped her lowered chin, bringing her eyes up to meet his, and kissed her.

"I think it's time we stopped dancing around each other," he said. "We're both AdultForms who know what we want—each other. I won't spend another minute pretending you're not the most captivating WomanForm I've ever seen, nor should you continue acting as if I don't matter. You know I'm in love with you, Lyric. I think it's time you allowed me to show you better than I can tell you."

She stood and caressed his face.

"I'm not due to report for duty until the week's first day. Let's see what you've got, Your Highness."

Clothes were shed as he planted kisses whenever her skin was revealed. She raised her arms so he could pull her dress over her head. Her kisses held all the pent-up passion she'd suppressed over the years.

Pulling her body closer to his chiseled frame, he lowered her to the floor of the craft. Arms locked around each other, they rolled over the floor of the craft, nibbling, sucking, and moaning in ecstasy. Positioning himself over her, he reached between her legs, parting her flesh to encircle the tight nub.

Giving it a gentle pinch and a soft tug, he replaced his fingers with his tongue. General Lyric thought she'd been flung to the moon when his hot, wet tongue flickered over her labia. She screamed as he sucked and licked between her folds. A rush of liquid flowed onto his lips, causing her to sit up in panic.

"Did I just urinate on you?" she cried.

He grinned up at her. "It's not what you think. It's natural."

Lowering his head, he feasted on her as if she were the last meal he'd ever have. Resting both hands on each side of his head, she threw back her head and moaned, shivering when his tongue traveled up her belly and encircled a taut nipple.

"Ohhhh," she said.

For what seemed like a sweet eternity, he used his tongue to lap, suck and tug at her breasts, sending her into a frenzy she never knew she was capable of. An unfamiliar feeling came over her when she felt heat rising and pulsing between her thighs.

"Prince Justin, do something!"

He scanned her beautiful face and laughed.

She opened her eyes, blinking at him in confusion. "What?"

He shook his head. "Lyric, how can you be so formal when I'm lying on top of you?"

She grinned, ducking her head into his shoulder. "I don't know. This is all so new to me!"

"You can call me anything you'd like—except that!"

Nibbling on her bottom lip he said, "I don't need the WomanForm I love to be anything except completely uninhibited with me."

"Alright."

"Mmmm... That's better. Now, what would you like me to do?"

"I feel like something is missing."

She pointed between her thighs. "Here."

Raising an eyebrow, he said, "Oh, there is. Let's see if you're ready," and slid a finger inside of her.

"Oh yeah, you're ready," he confirmed.

"For what?"

"Look at me," he commanded.

Her eyes fluttered open when he guided his long, thick shaft into her. Feeling pressure, her hands gripped his shoulders. There was a brief flicker of pain and then...pure bliss. She sighed when he thrust gently inside of her, slowly increasing the tempo as her body adjusted around him. He rode her faster, then harder.

"More! More!" she cried.

They rolled around on the floor, never breaking the tempo until sweat poured down his back. The timekeeper chimed, signaling an hour had passed before he covered her screams with his lips, thrusting his tongue into her mouth.

She rolled over again and found herself sitting atop him. Panting harshly, he threw back his head, guiding her in feverishly sliding up and down his shaft, now slick with her essence.

She pushed his face into her breasts, demanding more of his skillful, sensuous magic. He feasted on her nipples as if he were a dying man who'd just found a desperately needed antidote—her.

Sucking her tongue into his mouth drowned out her screams when they exploded and shot across Space with the stars. They made love a few more times before she fell across his chest, exhausted and panting for air. He pulled her close, kissing her forehead while running his fingers through her short, spiky hair.

"General, you are *amazing*!"

"I thought you said no formalities," she muttered and kissed his nipple.

"I did, but since I feel as if I've been on a battlefield for months, it's fitting."

Lifting her head, she frowned at him. "Did I hurt you?"

Cradling her bottom with his hand, he said, "No baby, but if you walk away from me again after what we've done here, you'll break my heart for good."

She rubbed her fingers over his bottom lip. "I have no intention of doing that."

She laid her head on his chest, encircling a nipple with her fingertip.

His manhood stirred against her thigh. "If you're telling me you want to go another round, give me a minute and I'll make it happen."

She groaned. "I'm too tired to move. I'll gladly take you up on your offer, but I think I'll need more than a minute. This was my first time, you know."

Pride swelled in him. Knowing he was her first lover pleased him. Immensely.

Her tone turned serious. "So now what do we do? Keep sneaking away to see each other?"

He swallowed hard, wrapping his arms around her waist. He wanted to ask her to marry him, but he knew it was impossible. She'd never give up her position to be with him. For now, returning to Earth wasn't an option either.

He'd grown to love JanIus too—his work and his patients mattered to him. And the mystery behind the strange dreams still plagued him. If King Carlomon were reaching out to him for help, he'd answer the call, even if it cost him his life.

"Come home with me. You don't have to go back for a couple more days. Spend the weekend with me."

Nibbling on his bottom lip, she said, "I thought you'd never ask, Your Highness."

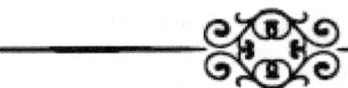

The smell of bacon and coffee enticed her out of a deep sleep. Sitting up straight in the firm, oversized bed, she winced. Their many rounds of passionate lovemaking came flooding back. She didn't remember when she'd felt so uninhibited.

That's what you get for being so greedy, she thought.

Justin entered carrying a silver tray stacked with fluffy scrambled eggs, crispy bacon, sage sausage, thick waffles dripping with maple syrup and butter, fruit salad, coffee, tea, and hot chocolate with melted marshmallows floating on top.

"Wait, I forgot something!" he said, setting the tray down next to her on the bed.

"Justin, if you add any more to this plate, someone will have to butter your doors and roll me out of here!"

He turned back to her and smiled. "You know, that's the first time you called me by my name? No 'Prince'?"

She blushed. "I'm sorry. My head has been all over the place since last night."

"Good to hear! Stay there and I'll be right back!"

"Where are you going?" she called out.

"It'll only take a second!"

As promised, he returned with a dozen white roses.

"There's a flower shop on the corner that delivers these. I meant to take them with me to the palace last night, but I forgot."

Smiling at her, he said, "I'm glad I did. This is much better."

"You mean with my DingoPops out in the open?"

He threw back his head and laughed. "So they're really called that?

"That's the slang term for them, yes. The formal term is breasts."

"Ms. Dill said you don't call them that here."

She stopped chewing on a piece of bacon. "Who is Ms. Dill?" she demanded.

He held up his hands. "She's just a patient—"

"A patient?!"

"Lyric, I didn't sleep with her! She told me that while I was examining her."

"You treat WomenForms?"

"It was either me or Dr. Azini. No one wanted him."

She groaned.

He raised an eyebrow. "You knew him?"

"I've heard of him. He was Fawn's father. From what she told me, he was a monster."

"He was, but please let's not waste the day talking about him."

Scooping up a small bit of eggs, she guided them to his open mouth. "Deal."

"Mmmm," he said, chewing vigorously. "Can we do this every morning?"

She smiled and kissed him on the lips. "You're so greedy, Dr. Ascencio!"

"Ah, but you were too last night!"

He laughed when she buried her face in his shoulder. "Come on, none of that! I like the out-of-control General Lyric. She's sexy!"

He never thought he'd hear her laugh again. It soothed his soul.

"Let's go out and explore the grounds today. King Leighton gave me a tour, but I didn't get to see everything."

"Let us go," she said. "If you're going to fit in here, get rid of the Human language."

He saluted her. "Yes, General."

"So everyone is okay with you being Queen Revari's son?"

He looked sheepish. "Well, that's the thing. I haven't revealed who I am yet. Not even to the king."

"Why?"

She listened as he told her about the dreams he'd had. "That's remarkable. What do you think he wants?"

Justin shook his head sadly. "I don't know. I wish I could put it all together. Once I do, I'll go back to Earth."

She turned her head to hide her sadness. Earth was where he belonged. As much as she wanted him to stay, she felt she had no right to ask him.

"Do you remember anything about Coldarius?"

She took another hefty bite of beef bacon. "I remember playing outside a lot. The weather was always cold, but we were happy. At least, Father and I were. Mother was hardly around."

She bit her lip. "I've forgotten what she looks like."

"What about your father? Any memories of him?"

"Of course. I'll never forget him as long as I live. My adoptive family told me they took me in when my ParentForms died."

But that isn't true, thought Justin. He knew at least General Iham was still alive when she was adopted. *Why had they lied to her?*

"Are there records of your adoption?"

"I've tried to access them in the Hall of Records, but they're sealed. Only two Beings I know have the security clearance to release them."

"Who?"

"Queen Vivant, of course. But I was surprised when the system listed another Being—General Gallium Barrios."

Swirling a piece of waffle in syrup, she said, "I won't get any answers from him. He hates me. I don't know why, and he won't tell me. He's older than I, so we never had classes together or ran in the same circles. I have no idea what I've done to offend him."

"He doesn't hate you," he assured her.

"How do you know? How well do you know him?"

"I don't think anyone knows him like General Legend and my mother. But he spoke very highly of your father. They served in Queen Dellah's army together. He has nothing but respect for General Iham."

"He told you that? Is that how you know my father's name?"

"Yes, he told me about him on Revani."

She ran her fingers through his hair, loving how its thick, silky texture felt against her skin. "Did he say anything about my mother?"

He cleared his throat. "Not much, other than she was his wife. I'm not sure how well he knew her."

He tried convincing himself that telling her the truth would break her heart. They'd just reconnected. There was no way he would spoil the blessing The One had sent his way. They ate in silence for a few moments.

"Are you up for taking a walk later?"

Her pensive expression made him pause. "What's the matter?"

"You say no one knows who you are. But if they see us together, they might start putting the pieces together. Then you may be outed."

She fed him a piece of bacon. "I don't think it would be a good idea. There's still a lot of prejudice against Humans—even half ones."

He pushed his plate aside. "You're probably right. Well, this cottage is quite a distance from town. King Leighton said he didn't put surveillance equipment around it, so we have all the privacy we need."

He looked around the spacious cottage. "There's an awesome recreation chamber with all kinds of things for us to get into."

Flicking her nipple with the tip of his tongue, he said, "When we get tired, we can come back here and entertain ourselves."

She nibbled on the last bit of sausage. "Sounds like a bargain to me. Let us clean up these dishes and take a shower."

"I'll take care of the dishes, you get in the shower. I'll join you in a minute."

She giggled. "How will we explore this fine cottage if you want to play in the shower all day?"

"All day? Oooh, I like the sound of that! Let us go!"

"Ah, see? You're already speaking like a true MaleForm. You take your lessons well, Your Highness."

"Mm. There's so more I'd like to learn from you, General," he said, stacking the dishes. Abruptly, he stopped.

She reached out and gently grabbed his arm. "What's the matter?"

"I, ummm...I should've brought this up last night, but I wanted you so badly. I don't have anything here to protect you."

She nodded toward her Azgoate sitting on the nightstand. "I think I'm covered."

"No, no. I don't mean weapons. I mean..."

Her eyebrow shot up. "Yes?"

"I don't have any condoms. I know it's too late to be crying about it now, but I feel I have a responsibility to protect you."

"What on Platirius are condoms?"

"They're slips of plastic that I place over my manhood. It's designed to catch my semen so you won't end up pregnant. They're not 100% foolproof, but having something is better than nothing. We're just getting to know each other. I don't think having a baby would be very smart."

Her cheeks puffed up. Then she laughed and laughed. He didn't know if he should be relieved or offended.

"May I ask what's so funny?"

She wiped tears from her eyes. "Oh, Justin. You're not on Earth. Set the dishes aside for a moment, please?"

She patted the space next to her. "Sit down."

In the throes of confusion, he sat next to her.

Taking his hand in hers, she said, "I'm not an expert on what Human women's bodies do, but I do know how ours work. We only become pregnant if we want to."

"What do you mean?"

"When sperm enters a WomanForm's womb, a substance called *Annilose* surrounds it. It holds it in a tiny bubble of fluid. When the bubble is formed, it creates a sensation she feels immediately. She determines if she wants it to travel to her eggs. If not, she dispels it from her body during an orgasm."

She squeezed his hand. "If the WomanForm doesn't have an orgasm, then the bubble passes through when she urinates. Either way, it stays until we decide where it goes."

Justin blinked at her. "So...is the...bubble... Did it leave when you had an orgasm?"

She nodded. "I dispelled it. I don't plan on being a wife and mother anytime soon. There are no unwanted or unplanned pregnancies in the galaxy. If an InfantForm is conceived, it is only with the free will of its mother."

He didn't know how to feel about that. He wasn't pining to be a father, but if he impregnated her, it wouldn't be the end of the world.

"I see," he said quietly.

"You just stated having a baby wouldn't be an intelligent thing to do. Why the long face?"

He squeezed her hand back. "I think I have a lot to learn about life in the galaxy."

"I agree. We have strict rules here. No children are born to unmarried ParentForms. Forced copulation is also against the law. On Platirius and Revani, any MaleForm who forces himself on a WomanForm is executed immediately. Is it that way for JanIus too?"

"I honestly don't know. I never thought to ask King Leighton about it."

"From what I've heard, he's a decent ruler," said General Lyric. "He doesn't seem like the type to allow WomenForms to go unprotected."

Justin nodded. He'd had enough lessons for the day. "I'm going to get these into the sanitizer and then we'll finish enjoying our time together, okay?"

She rubbed small circles on his muscular thigh. "Alright."

Admiring the view of his tight butt and thighs, she got up and entered the shower.

She let the gentle stream fall on her short curls. The change in his mood after she told him there would be no accidental pregnancy had confused her. His home was Earth. Hers was Platirius. They'd say their goodbyes once he solved the mystery of his strange dreams.

Wouldn't they?

King Belial lay on the floor of his war chamber, surrounded by artifacts, weapons, gold bars, silver, and jewels as far as the eye could see. Although he was one of the wealthiest kings in the galaxy, none of his possessions made him happy.

His nude form lay in a pile of sapphires and topaz. The sparkling jewels highlighted the gas blue hue of his iris. His dark red mane, falling past his shoulders, matched the line of hair traveling from his navel to nest around his thick, well-endowed member. Picking up a sapphire, he balanced it on his upright penis, watching it glisten under the moon's light.

"All of this could've been yours, Revari. Had you not turned your back on me."

King Belial's Past

She had returned! He ran up the hill at full speed to meet the lowering craft. She claimed she'd been trading off her sick father's possessions to feed herself. Enchanted by her beauty, he'd bought all of her wares.

He'd warned the other MaleForms to keep away when she visited. The closer he got to the craft, the more his excitement increased with his speed. Finally, he knew her identity. She had passed herself off as a poor commoner, desperately needing funds. That was a lie. He now knew her as—

"Princess Revari! It's nice to see you back on Platz."

She almost stumbled, but caught herself. Adjusting the thin, silk scarf covering her head, she strolled past him to set up shop.

"I have no idea what you're talking about, Prince Belial. I'm no more royalty than that whore peddling her body over there."

He laughed. "She may be a whore, but you're definitely a princess. My father recognized some of the things you sold. He threw a fit and ordered me to return them to the king, but we heard he's dying. Shouldn't you be taking care of him?"

Her long eyelashes and full curves made fire flicker in his lower region.

"You ask too many questions. Alright. You've discovered who I really am. Good for you. Are you going to buy something or not?"

He rubbed his hands together in anticipation. "It would be my pleasure. What do you have for me?"

She removed two expertly made daggers inlaid with mother of pearl and diamonds. Roaring pumas were carved onto the handles. He held his breath when she held up a petite blue topaz on a gold chain. He picked up the necklace, admiring its beauty in the light.

"This is almost as beautiful as you," he said, grinning at her. "I can't believe you'd part with it."

"I'm getting rid of everything he owns before my sister returns from training," she said, watching him inspect the necklace.

"He doesn't have long to live, and I don't want any reminders of him in my palace."

"Your palace?" he echoed. "So you think you, a WomanForm, will sit on the throne alone? You need a husband to be queen."

"The day I need a MaleForm for anything, I'll be buried next to my father's rotting corpse."

"What about Princess Vivant? General Kron might be dead, but she can easily marry a prince to take his place."

She blessed him with a stunning smile. "That won't happen."

"Why? She's still grieving the general?"

"Why are you so interested in my sister? Do you wish to take his place in her bed?"

"Oh no. I'm more interested in the princess standing in front of me."

She pushed the daggers toward him. "King Dubian had these made shortly before he married my Aunt Opal. You won't find anything finer in all of the galaxy."

He stared at her in awe before picking up one of the daggers to examine it. Noting an old, dark red stain on its tip, he said, "The blade is exquisite, and the handle... I've never seen anything like it."

Her lips pursed. "I told you," she sang.

"Alright, how much do you want for the necklace and the daggers?"

She quoted a price so high, he nearly cursed. But he could easily afford it, and she knew it.

"Done," he said, holding up his palm. When she held up hers, he quickly transferred the funds and snatched up his new treasures.

He tapped a small wooden box. "What do you have here?"

"My Aunt Opal's clothes. They're so plain and ugly, no one back home will take them."

His finger circled the lid of the expensive wooden box. "What about your mother's things? I'm sure they'd fetch a nice price."

Her eyes flashed like fire. "I'll never sell her belongings! The thought of my mother's gowns and jewelry on another WomanForm makes me ill."

He held up a hand. "Alright, calm down. I didn't mean to upset you."

"Don't tell me to calm down!"

A soldier approached her. "You will address the prince with respect!"

In a flash, the tip of her sword pressed against the soldier's neck.

"How dare you address me like a common WomanForm!"

The soldier raised his hands in the air, his wide eyes shifting quickly from her to the prince, who roared with laughter.

"It's alright, Captain Zion. She's Princess Revari of Platirius."

The soldier coughed and sputtered. "My apologies, Your Highness!"

"Silence, you animal," she said, lowering her sword. "Next time, mind your own business."

Bowing to her and the prince, he made a quick exit.

Grinning at her, Prince Belial said, "Ah, you'd make a wonderful queen. Sell the clothing to me. I have gardening staff who'll take them. Plain or not, they were worn by royalty."

After they made the final transaction, she got ready to leave, but he caught her hand.

"I know all about you. I heard how badly you were treated by your FatherForm, and you spent time in the Chamber of Despair. Your plans to take over Platirius won't make you happy.

Come and live here on Platz. Be my queen once my father passes."

She snatched her hand away, her eyes dancing with amusement.

"That didn't make me crazy enough to marry someone like you. You seem very impressed with yourself for discovering my identity. Now let me tell you what I know about you. You've killed more Beings than my father and General Kron combined."

Placing a hand on her hip, she said, "You don't mind forcing yourself on WomenForms either. Do you think my self-esteem is so low, I'd align myself with someone like you?"

His right eye twitched. "You lived with a Human. I don't think you have any room to judge me."

"He wasn't a murderer. He was a kind and decent Being. I'm not ashamed of loving him, but I wouldn't be able to show my face if I gave myself to a rapist."

He grunted. "Listen. I've never had to force myself on anyone. And second, no WomanForm has ever spoken to me that way."

"This WomanForm just did," she quipped.

He laughed and clapped his hands. "Ah, you have such fire, Princess Revari. I hear you're an efficient killer too. I won't judge you for being you. To me, you're perfect. I think we'd make a good team ruling Platz together."

"I think even though I might have been locked up, you're crazier than I'll ever be. Let it go, Prince Belial. In a thousand years from now, I still won't want you."

He smiled, watching the teasing sway of her lush hips storming off toward the craft.

"I'll never let it go, Princess. Not until you're mine," he promised.

Unaware the daggers and the CarogueStone she'd sold him were cursed, his mind became disoriented, causing his obsession with the princess to spin out of control. After King Dubian passed, he hounded her relentlessly, begging her to marry him.

On more than one occasion, he'd sit in his craft at the edge of Rubarius's borders, waiting for a glimpse of her. The Revaltians were on high alert, ready to blow him out of the sky if he crossed the Outer Realm.

He never did. He might've been crazy, but he wasn't stupid. The more she rejected him, the worse his insanity became.

He had never forced copulation on a WomanForm, but her accusation didn't bother him as much as her consistent rejection. No WomanForm had shunned his advances except her.

It tore his ego apart. He couldn't fathom not being good enough for her. In the end, he deluded himself into thinking she wanted him as much as he wanted her. Things took a downward spiral one fateful night.

Chapter 4

He had followed her and Gallium to a nightclub on a neighboring planet. Enraged by the handsome Coldarian MaleForm's presence, he challenged him to a duel.

Gallium scoffed before downing a drink. "I could kill you in the blink of a star, Prince Belial. But I respect your FatherForm too much to take his only son. You're drunk. Go home and sleep it off. Sober or not, Queen Revari will never take you for her husband, so collect what's left of your malehood and stop embarrassing yourself."

Queen Revari swirled the cherry in her glass and drained it. In an inebriated state, her words were heavily slurred.

"You see, Prince Belial? Even now, I wouldn't take you to my bed. When will you tire of your nonsense? Go home before you get hurt. Final warning."

"You don't want me because you think my eye wanders, is that it?"

She threw the cherry at him. "I don't want any part of you—eyes, ears, nose, or throat," she said.

Gallium and the rest of the patrons laughed. That made Prince Belial angry. Very angry.

"Why can't you see I'm in love with you?" he said. "What will it take to get through to you? Instead of taking my offer to rule Platz with me, you're sharing Platirius with your sister! Never before has a planet split. How perverted is that?"

She bristled. "I've earned my place on the throne. As for my sister, I'm taking care of that too, so don't you worry. As far as perversion, let's focus on you ogling my body. You think I don't know what you want? I'll never be your mindless bed whore!"

"If your right eye causes you to stumble, gouge it out and throw it away. For it is better for you to lose one part of your body than for your whole body to be thrown into hell!" he shouted.

Puzzled, she and Gallium looked at each other. "What on Platirius could that possibly mean?" she asked. "I hate to break it to you, but you're in a nightclub, not a worship chamber!"

The patrons laughed again, clearly enjoying the little show between the royals.

"Do you see your grandfather's face here?" he asked, pointing to his left eye.

She shook her head in disgust. "I have no idea what you're talking about! Grandfather Carlomon died when I was a baby. I have no memories of him."

He took a step toward her. "I can change that, My Queen. I can return everything you lost if you'll have me."

Gallium felt a chill go down his spine. "Coldarius was destroyed years ago. You're talking out of your ass! I won't tell you again. Leave now!"

"You're lying, Barrios!" he bellowed. His voice lowered to a whisper. "Coldarius is cursed. It won't let me rest unless I pluck it out!"

Before anyone could stop him, he removed one of the daggers he'd purchased from Queen Revari and plunged it into his right eye.

"Noooooo!" shouted Gallium, running toward him.

In horror, Queen Revari watched Prince Belial continue to stab himself in the eye, screaming obscenities. When Gallium reached for the dagger, evil magic blew him into the night sky.

He landed nimbly on his feet just before more patrons flung themselves on the prince, preventing him from hurting himself further.

The dagger lay a few feet away, his eye carefully positioned on the blade's sharp point. Miraculously, it was still intact.

A MaleForm retrieved the dagger and carefully laid it on his chest. He was still screaming her name when he was carried onto a craft hurtling swiftly toward the nearest medical chamber.

The Present

Bored with playing with the jewels, he got up and tossed them to the ground. The CarogueStone was hanging from his wardrobe's mirror.

Bewitched by its dark necromancy, he witnessed the fate of the Coldarians unfold again. Repeatedly watching them freeze to death and the king's murder had driven him further into madness.

"I love you, but I blame you," he whispered to the CarogueStone.

Carefully touching the mass of scars over his eyelid, he said, "You did this to me, Revari. You made me fall in love with you and enticed the spirits of your wretched family to haunt me. Why? Why curse me when I'm the only one who cares for you?"

He held the CarogueStone high in the air, the chain's golden glint matching the wicked gleam in his eye.

"Now it's time for the curse to return to you. Platirius has a male descendant. I know your half-Human son didn't die in the sun."

Violently shaking the stone, he said, "You could've borne a royal heir, yet you chose to lie with a filthy Human and produce an abomination! The time has come for your half-bastard to know pain."

He surveyed his nude form in the mirror. "And I'll be the one to introduce him to it."

Justin scanned his hand across the TeleShield of the medical chamber and smiled. He'd had a wonderful time with Lyric. He was looking forward to seeing her again. Balancing a stack of trays, Fawn nearly ran into him.

"Whoa," he said, stretching his hands to steady her. "What's with the trays?"

"One of the cleaning models didn't clear these out of the examination chambers last night. It broke down, and no one knew until this morning."

He took some of the trays from her.

"My father ordered it and fired dozens of cleaning staff. I've rehired them all. I don't want to depend on a machine and end up in a situation like this again."

Justin nodded. "Well, you're the boss. For what it's worth, I think it's a good idea."

As he stepped to move around her, she said, "I thought you'd be opposed to the idea."

"Why? I believe in Beings having jobs to support their families just as anyone else."

"I mean, I thought you'd take issue with my leadership."

"There's no reason for me to. King Leighton speaks highly of you. Anyone who successfully passed the queens' physician's program shouldn't be taken lightly. I'm here to help, not to antagonize you."

The anxiety that had mounted up inside of her instantly faded.

"Well, good. I'm glad to hear that. Then you won't have a problem with the changes I'll be implementing."

His eyebrow quirked. "And those would be?"

"Everything is detailed in the new program we're discussing today. If anyone has questions after the meeting, I've provided dates and times in the system to schedule a one-on-one meeting with me."

She balanced the trays in her hand. "Now if you'll excuse me, I need to get these to the dining chamber."

A group of cleaning staff bustled through the door just as she headed out.

"I'll get those, Dr. Azini," said Selma Hoardvak.

After retrieving the trays from Fawn, she marched them toward the dining chamber.

"Well, that's one thing I won't have to deal with," said Fawn. She nodded at Justin. "See you in a while, Dr. Ascencio."

"Alright, Dr. Azini."

Justin decided he liked the way she took charge. She was polite and professional—not irascible or disrespectful like her father. He looked forward to learning of her plans for the medical chamber.

After his acerbic first encounter with Thom Azini, he wasn't surprised his only daughter didn't seem upset over his death. Still, he hoped she wouldn't take anything out on him. He'd never wronged a female, nor was he planning to. He hoped she'd get to know him for who he was and not see him as just another MaleForm.

But why do you care what she thinks of you? he thought.

F awn closed the door to her office and wiped her sweaty palms on her pants. She hoped she hadn't made a fool of herself in front of Dr. Ascencio. She leaned her head back against the door.

Why do you care what he thinks of you?

"I don't," she said aloud.

And she didn't. At least...she hoped not.

J ustin quietly tapped his pen on the conference table while he waited for Dr. Azini's meeting began. Fawn stood in front of the head of the table. She thought wearing a crisp white blouse under a deep plum blazer would make her look confident.

The toes of her polished black heels peeked out from her wide-legged plum and lavender checkered slacks, which had gold threads running in a crisscross pattern through the heavy material.

She wore a simple amethyst stone on a slim gold chain around her neck and tiny gold hoops in her ears. Her fingers were free of rings. She didn't want to endure the daunting task of repeatedly taking them on and off between seeing patients.

On a whim, she'd purchased her first bottle of perfume at a boutique. When she carefully dashed a bit behind her ears and on her wrists, she smiled when the subtle, flowery scent filled her nostrils.

Her father hadn't allowed her and her mother to indulge in simple pleasures like perfume. Now that he was gone, she intended to have access to everything she'd been denied while he was alive.

Delighted with the staff provided by Revani and Platirius, she was overjoyed to meet with the department heads. They were gracious, hard-working, and genuinely seemed to care about the well-being of others.

"I'd like to thank everyone for coming today. If you haven't had breakfast yet, please help yourself to some refreshments."

She was proud of the table she'd set. A white platter of thick slices of cheese pie and glazed doughnuts sat next to a large, white bowl of colorful fruit salad. A platinum carafe of coffee stood next to crystal pitchers of freshly squeezed orange juice and a delightful pomegranate juice.

The platinum pitcher of cream, a bowl of sugar, tall crystal tumblers, white mugs, hexagon-shaped white plates, and platinum silverware made a beautiful picture against the lavender tablecloth and napkins. After she added purple roses and white lilies in short, crystal vases, she thought the table looked perfect.

She watched her colleagues pass around the food and prepare their drinks.

"The dining staff baked everything fresh this morning," she offered, nervously rubbing her hands together. She noted they were dry. That was good. The last thing she wanted was to be a bundle of nerves on her first day.

When she waved her hand across the air, *Welcome* appeared above their heads. She hoped to emulate Captain TamRi's easygoing technique.

"Now that everyone has been served, let's go around the table and introduce ourselves. No need to stand. I want you all to feel comfortable as we get to know each other better."

A beautiful WomanForm with dark hair and hazel-green eyes had just bitten into her slice of cheese pie. Her cheeks puffed up with laughter when she noticed she was first. She quickly picked up a napkin and covered her mouth until she'd finished chewing.

"Sorry, it looked really good and I skipped breakfast to make sure I was on time for the meeting!"

"It's okay," said Justin. "It *is* good. I'm trying not to get another slice after I polish this one off."

Her merry eyes sparkled. "Anything that tastes this divine has to be good for us, right?"

Justin winked at her. "Of course!"

Her bubbly laughter caused all of them to join in. Fawn liked her immediately.

"I'm Dr. Jessica Chirp. I'm a heart specialist from Platirius. I've worked under Queen Vivant's authority when her half was Platineous, and since her daughters were ChildForms. I have two birds, Mercedes and Cervantes. I'm happily married and have a small daughter, who is five summers."

"Welcome, Dr. Chirp," said Fawn. "If Queen Vivant sent you, I suspect you'll be a wonderful asset to the team. I'm thrilled to have you with us."

"Thank you very much, Dr. Azini. I'm happy to be on JanIus and to be a part of this team," said Dr. Chirp.

Next up was a MaleForm with smooth, brown skin who wore slim, wire-frame glasses.

Taking a sip of coffee, he smiled and said, "Well, I guess I'm next."

His easy-going smile instantly made his colleagues feel at ease.

"I don't have birds or anything, but my name is Dr. Clint, and I'm an MD. Now, that doesn't mean mimosas and daiquiris. I wish."

He chuckled when a round of laughter broke out again.

"I've been practicing for about five hundred years, but as long as I don't look it, I can go five hundred more!"

Justin raised his glass to Dr. Clint. "Hear, hear!"

Everyone toasted to Dr. Clint, who raised his hands and smiled.

Next up was a tall, voluptuous WomanForm with long dark hair pulled into a severe bun. Her coppery skin looked as if it had been kissed by the sun.

"I'm Dr. Holler-Managan. I am a Neurology InfantFormatrician from Akron."

Dr. Clint whistled. "Planet Akron is a long way from here."

Dr. Holler-Managan nodded. "It is, and I was happy to pack up and leave. I was the only WomanForm on the team, and things weren't as pleasant as I would've liked them to be."

Fawn silently applauded her.

"But that's all over. Now I'm here on JanIus. I get to work with cute InfantForms all day and listen to them tell me about their problems. I love my work and what I do. The only thing that gets me upset is if a mysterious illness pops up that I can't get rid of."

She added cream and five lumps of sugar to her coffee. "But thanks to our advancements in medicine, it doesn't take us long to find cures. That makes me very happy."

"Welcome, Dr. Holler-Managan," said Fawn.

Dr. Charlyce Wallington was next. "I'm also an InfantFormatrician. I'm originally from Akron, but I was on Pletz before it merged with Platirius. I also worked under Queen Vivant."

Justin assumed she was nervous when she paused to look down at her hands.

"I volunteered to come to JanIus when I heard there were a lot of MotherForms who needed care for their InfantForms. I don't think I'd be happy doing anything else. I'm very pleased to meet all of you."

After they welcomed her, Dr. Corning, a general practitioner, introduced himself, followed by Dr. Barbara, a mental wellness physician.

"I'm happy to note that mental wellness has improved within the last 10,000 years. We used to lock Beings away to ensure they weren't a danger to themselves or others. That was considered good medicine when I first started. Now that's no longer the case. We only institutionalize Beings as a last resort."

She adjusted her name tag. "I think it's a heartless, barbaric thing to do when we have so many new and innovative avenues to treat the mind. Science has made significant contributions to galactic medical research.

Justin shifted in his chair. Queen Revari had shared she'd been institutionalized after she thought he'd died. He couldn't imagine the pain she'd experienced being locked away for years.

"Through therapy and education, we teach Beings to live with the consequences of decisions. Suffering shouldn't go unnoticed. Beings should have a fierce circle of support and know they are loved and cared for. I hope that aligns with your vision, Dr. Azini."

"It does, Dr. Barbara." She nodded at Justin. "We have one more."

Justin cleared his throat. "I'm Dr. Ascencio. I'm a neurosurgeon with a dual license in internal medicine. Since I know a lot about the brain, I could probably bore you to tears talking about it, so I won't."

He grinned. "I've enjoyed meeting some of the most engaging Beings I've ever seen in my lifespan. My theory is that if you do something you love, it'll never feel like work. I've enjoyed working here and hope to continue for as long as you'll have me."

He nodded at Fawn. "Thank you."

"Thank you, Dr. Ascencio," said Fawn. "Well, I guess it's time to introduce myself. I am Dr. Fawn Azini. I'm a ParaNurture physician and the head of this medical chamber. My job will be delivering and overseeing the care of InfantForms. I designed and commissioned a new wing to be built specifically for pregnant MotherForms and it was completed yesterday."

She clasped her hands together. "I plan to work with all of you very closely, and I have a few changes I'd like to make."

When she waved her hand again, *Welcome* was replaced by a series of text.

"For years, JanIus's medical chambers were numbered and that's what Beings referred to them as. Numbers. Well, the problem with that is numbers shouldn't be connected to Beings unless it's for identification—birth dates, craft license numbers, etc."

She paused to wipe her palms on her pants. "In this chamber, we take care of Beings. So it's only natural the chamber should have the name of a Being instead of a number. You probably saw the building staff putting up a new sign out front. Starting today, this medical chamber will be called The Azini Institute for Wellness."

"That's nice of you to name it after your FatherForm," said Dr. Barbara.

Fawn shook her head. "It's not named for him—I named it after me."

Dr. Barbara looked sheepish. "Oh. I'm sorry."

"No, don't be. The name is a tangible reminder that change can be beautiful and uplifting. I want this chamber to be known around the galaxy for having exceptional practitioners who care about their patients. My vision for this practice is to provide top notch care for every JanIan. We're small, but we've never been in last place, and I don't intend to start now."

Looking around the room, she focused on each of their faces. "My father is dead, and with him died years of ignorance and cruelty. I refuse to tolerate it from my staff and the patients. So, if any patient comes here with a threat of violence and they're not experiencing a mental health crisis, they will be removed from the grounds immediately."

The physicians followed the text when she waved her hand.

"I've secured King Leighton's permission to remove the internal cameras. Since I'm taking over, they won't be needed anymore. However, I kept the ones outside for added security."

She perused the list carefully. "Let's see, what do I have next? Ah! It's important to me that the WomenForms have access to female staff."

She turned to Justin. "Dr. Ascencio, I know you've been helping out and taking them on as patients, but if you're more comfortable with MaleForms, I can arrange it."

"That won't be necessary. As long as my female patients want me to treat them, I'm good seeing either SexForm," said Justin.

"Okay, good," said Fawn. "Moving on, lunch breaks are now mandatory. I believe Beings perform better when properly nourished, so when it's your turn, please take your luncheon break off the grounds. Get out, breathe some fresh air, and have a good meal so you can return refreshed and ready to assist our patients."

Pausing to refill the pitcher of grape juice, she said, "Our dress code has changed too. I'm working with Tese Blight to design our uniforms. She's the granddaughter of Marcia Blight. She assured me they'll be finished by the end of the month. Each of you will receive seven uniforms and seven white coats. The laundry staff will clean and press them each week at no cost to you."

Tese Blight was one of the most famous fashion designers in the galaxy.

Dr. Chirp did a little dance with her shoulders. "I've never been dressed by a celebrity before," she said.

Fawn smiled. "I've known Tese for a long time. She has impeccable taste in fashion."

Dr. Clint looked at everyone and said, "We're going to look like we're fresh from the club when we come to work!"

Everyone laughed except Fawn, who had never seen the inside of a club in her lifespan.

"You'll be dressed well without smelling like spirits," she said primly. "And that leads me to the last thing on the agenda. This is a smoke-free and drug-free building. I know that sounds a bit off, considering it's a medical chamber."

Justin observed how she neatly she stacked the dishes and leftovers onto a small cart.

"What I mean is, no recreational drugs are allowed on the premises. As for the drugs we used to treat patients, all are under a brand-new security system. The supply closet has been updated with a new TeleShield. You'll be required to scan your palms each time you prescribe or administer drugs to Beings."

A stunned silence permeated the room. Except for Platirius, the chambers where most of the physicians previously worked didn't require scanning to access drugs.

"If you'll raise your palms, I'll provide you with a list of banned drugs. The most lethal is Callidut. It's never to be used without prior authorization from Queen Revari. If I see it, the Being will be arrested and hauled off to the confinement chamber until they have their day in front of the justice council. Does anyone have any questions?"

No one raised their hand.

Fawn nodded. "Good. I look forward to working with all of you. I'll make my rounds to each of your departments once a month for supervision checks."

Finally, the table had been cleared. "I don't believe in micromanaging my staff. You're some of the best medical professionals in the galaxy and I trust all of you to provide excellent care. If there's ever a time when you experience burnout, my door is always open."

She clapped her hands together softly. "Our meeting is adjourned. I'll let you get on with your day."

Justin stood up and stretched. "I can take those dishes over to the dining chamber if you want, Dr. Azini."

"That won't be necessary. The cleaning staff will pick them up. After hours, Farah 2000 will take over their duties until morning. Thank you for offering."

He nodded at her. "One of the newer models? Well, that's convenient. I heard it communicates very well."

"It does. I met it at school. Farah 2000 has a very pleasant personality."

"Well, I'm looking forward to seeing it around. See you later."

"In a while," she said to him.

He opened the door and paused.

Where have I heard that phrase before?

King Asa poured another glass of peach cognac. He looked up as King Belial entered, unannounced. On alert, he looked over his unwanted guest's shoulder.

Raising his hands in a mock surrender, King Belial said, "I've come alone."

Seeing King Asa's hand go under his shirt, he said, "Don't worry, I haven't killed anyone. No need to be on guard."

"You just walked into my palace as if you own it. Do you expect me to be at ease?"

"Of course!" said King Belial, grabbing a fresh glass and helping himself to the bottle. He quickly downed the drink, licking his lips with satisfaction. "Ah! I swear, Onzi has the best spirits."

King Asa studied the eye patch nestled carefully on his right eye before shifting to the electrifying energy burning in his left.

"What do you want, King Belial?"

"Now, is that any way to talk to an old friend?"

King Asa scoffed. "Friends? We went to the same instruction chambers but never hung out in the same circles. You were always...a bit too vulgar for my tastes."

King Belial sneered. "And you always acted as if you'd get dirty if the Platzians mingled with the Onzians for too long."

His winsome smile didn't reach the coldness in his eye. "As if we were insects whose sole existence rested on having the honor of being crushed under your foot."

A soldier burst through the door. "King Asa! Surveillance alerted me that King Belial—"

King Asa looked pointedly at King Belial then at the soldier.

"I'm sorry, My King, had I known he was here, I would've—"

King Belial's baleful eye stared at the soldier. "You would've what?" he asked softly.

His smile chilled the soldier, but he met the king's stare without flinching.

"We would've stopped you from entering His Majesty's doors," he said flatly.

King Belial sighed. "Stopped me," he whispered. "They would've stopped me."

Taking out an Azgoate, he fired at the soldier's head, sending his brain flying to the floor with a sickening *splat*.

"Belial!" King Asa bellowed. "What do you mean coming here and shedding blood on my floors?"

A group of soldiers rushed into the private dining chamber.

"What the hell good is it to come now?!" yelled King Asa. "He's already killed Corporal Bonan!" Furiously, he waved his hand. "Just get him out of here and dispatch the cleaning staff to get up the blood before it seeps into my floor!"

More soldiers ran in and stationed themselves behind King Belial.

King Belial whistled. "No need to bring in the whole army. I'm just here because I'm thirsty."

King Asa whirled around to glare at him. "Your thirst for blood never quenches! Maybe you didn't know this, but the spirits of Beings who meet untimely deaths roam my grounds until they receive vengeance! I trust you won't inconvenience me further with your nonsense, Belial! He was no threat to you!"

King Belial hadn't stopped smiling since he arrived. "Are you?"

Exasperated, King Asa sighed. "Have I ever visited Platz? Even once?"

King Belial sat back in the chair, pretending to think. "You know, now that you've said something, I don't remember you reaching out to me. Not even after I had my accident."

King Asa poured another drink. He had a feeling he'd need it.

"For what? To tell you to stop pining over King Dubian's youngest daughter? She spent years in the Chamber of Despair and hasn't allowed a MaleForm to touch her since her father got rid of that ignorant Human husband of hers."

Pointing at King Belial, he said, "What did you think was going to happen? She'd look into the gaping hole in your head and fall madly in love with you? I don't think even she is that crazy!"

"Shhhh, you're hurting my feelings, Asa," said King Belial, filling his glass again with the sweet, peach liquor. "I like to think I'm still a handsome MaleForm."

King Asa's fierce scowl darkened his handsome face. "You're straight from Hell, Belial."

King Belial slid a lone finger down the cool glass. "You say such sweet things."

"What do you want from me?" asked King Asa.

"We haven't had supper yet, and already you're asking me what I want."

"Forgive me for losing my appetite after looking at all the blood you've spilled."

"You can't drink your problems away, Asa. Research proves it."

"What the hell do you know about research, Belial? You've never been interested in studies."

"I am now."

"Really? Humor me. Why?"

"I want to know all there is to know about doctoring."

King Asa looked to the guards.

"Now at least hear me out before I hurt a couple more of your soldiers. I only came to talk, Asa. Not for violence."

"It's too late for that now, isn't it?" roared King Asa.

"Come now. There's no need to be rude. You're a MaleForm of class and reason, aren't you?"

King Asa prayed to The One for patience. "Tell me what you want. Then leave."

"I just told you. I want to know about medical things."

"And why the sudden interest in that?"

"Don't you have a new WomanForm doctor assigned here?"

"Yes. All the planets have been receiving female physicians, except for yours." King Asa rubbed his beard. "I can't say I'm surprised. Queen Revari wants you dead so she can absorb Platz."

The smile finally disappeared from King Belial's face. "That'll never happen. And speaking of Queen Revari... Did you hear she has a half-Human son running around JanIus wiping the noses of Beings?"

Chapter 5

King Asa set down his glass with a hard *thump*. "What?"

King Belial rubbed his hands together. "She has a bastard son. His Human name is Dr. Justin Ascencio, but his real name is Prince Justin Ascencio-Carogue-Amorous."

King Asa's mind was racing rapidly. King Belial was insane, there was no doubt about that. But was he a liar?

"A male heir to Platirius is here in the galaxy?"

"Mmhmm. Isn't that depressing?"

King Asa took a step back from the table. "What does he want? The throne?"

"No. He hasn't tried to take it."

Easing his body slowly into the chair, King Asa asked, "But what about the power that comes with it?"

King Belial cracked his knuckles. "According to some of my discreetly placed staff, he claims he isn't interested in becoming a king."

"Then what does he want? And why is he here?"

"He says he wants to heal Beings. Nothing more. As for the second part of your question, I'll need food before we continue. My energy is winding down fast."

King Asa scowled at him before nodding to a soldier. "See to it," he ordered.

"But you haven't asked me what I wanted to eat!" said King Belial.

"Do you think you're at a new pub?"

"I think," said King Belial slowly, "if you keep talking crazy to me, I'm gonna reach over and rip your voice box out of your neck. Now a few of your soldiers might get a few jabs in, but we both know I can kill all of them and still reach around, slice off your cock and put it in your mouth, yes?"

King Asa leaned forward, pointing a finger in his face. "You get this straight. Half the galaxy might be afraid of you, but I'm not. Come for me and I'll take your head clean off. And you can you put that on your dead whore of a mother!"

King Belial drummed out a song on the desk with his knuckles. "Don't talk badly about my mother, Asa. She was a good WomanForm."

"She left you with your FatherForm two months after birthing you to slide under King Hitam. And after he was done with her, he passed her around like a deck of cards to his soldiers. She allowed him to play with her mind for twelve years before it finally dawned on her that he was never going to marry her."

King Belial's tune slowly faded out.

"After she tried to disrupt his wedding, she was tossed out of the worship chamber before crashing her craft into the cliffs your palace sits on. She self-destructed because King Hitam didn't want her. Does that sound familiar?"

King Asa reared back in his chair. "I had a lot of respect for your father. He was a kind and rational king who treated his subjects fairly. You? I don't think her genes ever gave you a chance to be normal."

"Normal doesn't exist," said King Belial. "Everything and everyone is abnormal."

"So Queen Revari has a son who doesn't want the throne. But he's in the galaxy to practice medicine when he could do it on Earth. Does that make sense to you?"

"No," said King Belial. "But it doesn't matter. I intend to behead him right in front of her."

"You want to kill her son? Why?"

"I want him dead because she slid under a Human instead of me. Once he's gone, she'll see we can still be together."

He raised one hand in the air. "No, Asa. Hush. Hear me out. Once he's gone, she and I can have a purebred son. One who'll sit on Platirius's throne."

King Asa raised an eyebrow, then rubbed a hand over his weary eyes. "How do I fit into this madness?"

"I need a cover. I want to apply for a work pass on JanIus, but I can't go looking like this."

"You intend to use your powers to change your appearance."

"Yes." He gave King Asa an admiring glance. "You always were the smartest MaleForm in class."

King Asa glanced at the retreating cleaning staff, who had finished getting up Corporal Bonan's blood before rushing out of the den.

"Why should I help you? What's in it for me?"

King Asa paused as his dining staff spread a black tablecloth over his desk and quickly set a small feast in front of them.

King Belial gazed appreciatively at the colorful platters of jerk chicken and pork, fried plantains, brown stew chicken, rice and peas, and oxtail stew. For dessert, rum cake and a large bowl of fresh fruit were served.

In another time, King Asa had spent his training on Earth and developed a fondness for Jamaican cuisine. He glowered at King Belial, who was happily digging into the food.

"I hear you're fond of Queen Vivant," said King Belial.

King Asa's eyes narrowed. "She's none of your business."

"Does she want you too?" asked King Belial, taking a hefty bite of the oxtail stew.

King Asa's teeth began grinding—a sign he was being pushed too far. "Stay out of my business, Belial."

The soft warning made King Belial smile again. "Her husband has been gone for a long time. A beautiful WomanForm with a face and body like that, sleeping all alone. Tsk. If you ask me, it's just criminal!"

Not missing the slight emphasis on *criminal*, King Asa sat up straighter. "If you harm a hair on her head..." he warned.

King Belial forked up some rice and peas. "Asa! What kind of Being do you think I am?!"

"I know exactly what you are—less than an animal. That's why I'm telling you to stay away from her. She's had enough to deal with over the years. She doesn't need you making things worse."

A wicked light shone in King Belial's eye. "You really are in love with her, aren't you?"

King Asa's stare was deadly calm. "You may believe your insanity gives you leverage over the rest of us, but it doesn't. If you touch her, I won't hesitate to kill you and take Platz." He snorted. "Your soldiers would thank me."

"No one has to die if you provide the work pass and recommendation I need to go to JanIus.

"She has an entire army to protect her. And so do I."

He stopped short at an object King Belial withdrew from his pocket and held up into the light.

"What's that?"

"One of her bras." He put it up to his nose. "Mmmm. Smells like candy. I must say, the Amorous queens have the biggest DingoPops this side of the galaxy!"

King Asa's jaw tightened.

"Does it look familiar? You gifted it to her last year." King Belial tapped the price tag. "She's never worn it."

Rage surged through King Asa. "How did you get it?"

"I just went into her bed chamber and took it. She has a very peaceful face when she's asleep."

King Asa jumped out of his seat. "You—"

King Belial held up a piece of jerk chicken. "Now, now. No need to get mad. I haven't harmed her." He watched King Asa's enraged face change color. "Or her daughters," he added. "And I won't."

He popped the chicken in his mouth, chewing enthusiastically. "But you should know, I have a little gift that lets me transport in and out of places without being seen. That's why your guards didn't spot me until I arrived."

He placed the bra on the side of King Asa's plate. "Let's be friends, Asa. Give me what I need to finally have the WomanForm I love, and I promise I'll leave Queen Vivant alone."

"You'll leave her alone regardless. I have no reason to trust you."

"I'm many things, but a liar isn't one of them. I pride myself on telling the truth."

King Asa glared at him. He wished he could put him out of his misery, but King Belial was one of the greatest fighters born into the Arturo dynasty. For all of his wickedness and idiosyncrasies, he was a very efficient killer. He couldn't take the chance that Belial would take his head and hurt Queen Vivant.

He's found another evil source that gives him a cover to roam where he pleases.

He studied King Belial as a predator monitors its prey. "You know, I didn't become king by being a coward or a follower. I am the youngest son out of three males. My father didn't believe I could successfully run Onzi. I had to prove it to him after Queen Aiki murdered both of my brothers."

King Belial groaned in delight after sampling the plantains. "And how did you prove it?"

"I slit his bastard daughter's throat right in front of him. He was having supper just as you are now. I made sure the blood dripped into his bowl of tomato bisque."

King Belial's vigorous chewing slowed.

Meeting his eyes, King Asa said, "But then...you know all about bastard daughters, don't you?"

King Belial swallowed and licked his lips. Slowly.

"The ChildForm was never proven to be mine."

King Asa's light gray eyes were bathed in hatred. "Had you been my brother, my father would've punished you for shaming his name. But your father was too kind. He doted on you—repeatedly overlooking your blatant disrespect for his throne."

Calmly folding his hands on the table, he said, "I see I finally have your full attention. You thought you'd come here and dangle a WomanForm I'm fond of over my head, but you didn't calculate I knew your business too."

King Belial sat perfectly still. Waiting.

Coiled like a snake, thought King Asa.

"Your daughter has been living a lie. She never knew her parents or how she came to be. To avoid punishment for siring a bastard, you've allowed her to be raised in poverty instead of royalty. You speak of love as if it's something you're familiar with, when in reality, your heart is about as empty as the space between Heaven and Hell."

He pointed at King Belial's face. "That's the real reason Queen Revari will have nothing to do with you. She's not about to align her legacy with a king with no sense of responsibility or self-control."

King Belial's eye glittered dangerously. "You have no right to judge me."

"You walked into my home and asked for it. I believe in giving Beings what they deserve. So let me make it plain for you. Moving forward, my surveillance team's duties will be increased to provide extra protection to Queen Vivant. If I so much as hear you entered her palace just to break wind and leave, I'll hunt your daughter down and slit her throat on the steps of your palace."

King Asa picked up his glass and poured the rest of his cognac over the jerk chicken, rice and peas and plantains on King Belial's plate.

"Now get your despicable ass out of my realm. And don't return."

King Belial frowned at the plate. "You didn't let me finish my meal, Asa. How rude."

"Would you like your daughter to finish her lifespan?"

King Belial grinned. "What's to stop me from killing the ChildForm and Queen Vivant?"

"You won't," King Asa countered. "You've secretly provided funding to her over the years. I know all about King Noham's secret little visits to the orphanage where she grew up. Her eyes are the same color as his."

The glass clinked sharply on the desk when he set it down. "As insane and bloodthirsty as you are, perhaps there's something inside that dark, empty heart of yours that beats for her. It could be pity, considering who her mother was. Maybe you did her a favor by not claiming her. I imagine growing up with you as a FatherForm would've been horrendous."

King Belial broke off a piece of rum cake with his hands instead of cutting it.

"I'm not giving you a pass to kill Queen Revari's son. King Leighton hasn't done anything to me, so there's no reason to disrespect his realm by helping you trespass. My focus is to learn everything about this half-Human and see how close he is to Queen Vivant. If he isn't, then I'll eliminate him, and the threat of conquering Platirius will end. Why should I give you that kind of advantage over me?"

King Belial used his finger to trace a DeathCraft on the tablecloth. No trace of the jovial playfulness he initially exuded remained. "You're not playing by the rules, Asa."

King Asa laughed bitterly. "No, I'm just not as dumb and vulnerable as you thought I was. I always have an ace up my sleeve, and I keep it sharp enough to cut teeth on." He stood up, beyond weary of the Platzarian's presence. "I don't know where you'll get your little work pass, nor do I care. Just steer clear of Platirius." He nodded toward his soldiers.

King Belial sighed. "Fine. I'm leaving. I have the pass anyway."

"I'm not surprised. You came here to irritate me and put me on notice that a Human has infiltrated our borders." He inclined his head toward King Belial. "Thank you, but no thank you. I intend to rule Platirius with Vivant by my side. And no Being—half royalty or not—will get in my way."

The two kings stared each other down for a moment. One was considerably taller than the other, but only one had a sane mind and spine of steel.

"I'll be seeing you, King Asa," promised King Belial, strolling toward the entrance.

"Not before I see your daughter."

King Belial paused at the threat in his tone.

"She works for me now. A strange name she has...Domi."

J ustin whistled while he cleaned off the counter and got ready for lunch. He rubbed his hands in anticipation of eating at a new shopping outlet that had just opened. He loved JanIus's fast-paced scene.

Unlike the communal dining chambers steeped in historical value on Platirius and Revani, JanIus had a variety of cafes, clothing boutiques, and nightclubs. Except for the different scenery, it looked like life on Earth might have been if it were in the year 5050.

He agreed with King Leighton's plans to keep JanIus youthful and innovative. Not knowing when or if he wanted to return to Earth, he put it out of his mind and focused on the new life he was building.

His TeleScreen chimed sharply just before he left the door. He smiled when he read the name flashing across the screen.

"Well, hello, beautiful! This is a surprise!"

"Hi," said General Lyric. "I have a few minutes before Captain Kourtney and I have field duty, and wanted to see how you were."

"I'm fine and how are you?"

Smiling, she twisted the chain around her neck. "Have you been taking care of yourself? I know you're dedicated to healing others, but you were hurt not so long ago. You should be eating well and getting lots of rest."

"Ah, I've been a good MaleForm. I'm not pushing myself too hard."

"Good, because you scared me to death. I didn't like seeing you lying in a medical bed."

"Well, I made up for it when I took you to mine, didn't I?"

General Lyric grinned, then blushed. "You're incorrigible."

I'm in love with you.

He didn't say it aloud out of fear she wouldn't say it back.

"So what are you doing tomorrow? It's the end of the week, you know? Will my aunt have you running back and forth across the galaxy?"

She closed her eyes, still smiling. "No, but if her nephew is nice to me, I might fly over and spend some time with him."

He nearly dropped the TeleScreen. "Are you serious?"

Amused, she said, "Do I know how to joke?"

She laughed when he groaned. "No, but there's hope for you yet, Lyric! I'd love for you to come here and be with me. I'll have everything planned. Just show up, okay?"

She nodded at his pleased expression. "Okay. Should I bring anything special?"

"Hmm... Do you have any shorter dresses?"

She frowned. "No. I don't think so. Why?"

"What size are you? No. Don't tell me. I think I can guess."

"You can guess?" she echoed doubtfully. "How?"

"Lyric, I've held everything of yours in my hands...and my mouth."

"Oooh!" said Captain Kourtney. "Looks like I walked in on something private. I'll be waiting for you at the gate, General."

Blushing furiously, General Lyric gave her the okay sign.

"Er, sorry," said Justin. "Like I said, I know every inch of your body. Just bring yourself and any personal toiletries you want. I'll take care of everything else."

"Sounds like a deal. I should be there by eight," she said.

His green eyes sparkled. "I can't wait."

"It should be luncheon time there. Have you eaten?"

"Not yet. I'm on my way to try out a new cafe."

"Captain TamRi and Major Thea told me JanIus has some really cool places."

"Yeah, King Leighton is young and wants to liven it up a bit. I'm all for it. Listen, I'll see you when you get in, okay?"

Her violet-gray eyes flashed with mischief. "You mean when *you* get in."

His mouth dropped. "General Lyric! Did you just tell a dirty joke?"

She covered her mouth and laughed. "Sergeant Alicia taught that one to me."

"Oh wow! I'll have to pick her up a gift and send it back with you! My WomanForm has a sense of humor!"

Her expression turned serious. "Is that what I am to you? Yours?"

"I hope so. My heart would break into a million pieces if you didn't want to be."

He loved her smile.

"No need for that. I'm fine with it. Now go on and get some grub! I'll see you soon."

"Alright, love. See you soon."

Dr. Clint appeared as he disconnected the transmission.

"Looks like someone has something hot and heavy coming up!"

Justin turned and said, "Hey, Dr. Clint! Yeah, my...lady is coming to see me."

"Ohhh, look at you! You sly dog! And here I thought you were dating a few of the female NurseForms here. They draw straws sometimes to see who'll get you."

That surprised Justin. He hadn't noticed anyone noticing him.

"No, I don't believe in mixing business with pleasure. Besides, I already consider myself taken. Are you headed out to eat?"

"Yeah. I'm in the mood for a good fish sandwich, cabbage slaw, and fried chips."

"Let's try the new cafe that opened across from the institute and see if the food is worth it."

Dr. Clint nodded. "Sounds like a plan, Dr. A! Let us go!"

On their way to the cafe, neither noticed a cleaning staff sweeping trash into a compost bin. Keeping his head lowered, he didn't nod at the doctors as they passed. A baby bird, caught in the pile, was desperately trying to escape from the bin.

Focusing on the small creature with a single eye, he said, "Let me help you," before reaching inside and breaking its neck.

Queen Vivant adjusted her wide-brimmed hat and gathered a few of the heirloom tomatoes she'd planted into her basket.

"That's quite a hat you have there," said a low baritone voice.

She turned and found King Asa smiling at her.

"Asa? This is a surprise. We won't meet to discuss Domi's progress until next week."

Those gray eyes and long eyelashes. Just like—

"I know, but I wanted to see you."

An amused brow lifted. "Why?"

"You know why, My Queen."

Rising to her full height, she looked down at the headstrong king.

"You're not my servant or my husband. You shouldn't call me that."

His next words stopped her in her tracks. "How long will you ignore how I feel about you?"

She turned to face him again. "My husband is dead. So is my mother, grandfather, and aunt. And yet," she said, looking up at the sun, "The One heard my prayers. I finally have the daughters I thought I lost to Death. There's no room in my life for any other Being, Asa. Now that you've heard me say it aloud, maybe you'll take it to heart."

"Am I just supposed to forget how you felt in my arms that night?"

She bit her lip. "I had a weak moment. I had never been with another MaleForm besides my husband. Are you going to hold that against me?"

He shook his head in amazement. "Vivant, there's nothing to hold against you. We made love. It's impossible to cheat on a dead MaleForm. There's no shame in moving on with your life."

"My daughters—"

"Are fully grown now. They're no longer TeenForms."

She grinned at him. "TeenForms. Is that the new language out of JanIus?"

He smiled back at her. "I admit King Leighton's progressive new ways and language have become popular. I think JanIus livens up the galaxy, don't you?"

She had to agree. The princesses had spent more time partying than learning how to manage a queendom, but she wasn't complaining. They were young and intelligent. And thanks to her sister, very skilled in warfare. She looked forward to the day when one of them would take the responsibility of claiming the throne, but not for a long time.

"We're not old, you know?" said King Asa. "We have too many years left before we sit on the balcony, yelling at the ChildForms to stay off the grass."

His heart sang when she laughed out loud. He never tired of hearing her laugh. Not wanting to make her feel crowded, he pointed to the tomatoes. "What are those for?"

She looked at the bundle proudly. "I'm going to make tomato bruschetta."

"I don't think I've had it."

"Oh, it's delicious. I make a wonderful cream cheese, chive, and bacon spread for it."

"Sounds good." His tone suggested the bruschetta wasn't the only thing he wanted to sample.

She took in his wavy black hair, goatee, and muscular form. He wasn't short. He simply wasn't as tall as she. If she let go of General Kron, she might be able to entertain his advances.

Her daughters had grown up without their father, but she still couldn't forget the wonderful times they'd shared. Now that they had their own lives and didn't need her as much as they once did, loneliness had slowly crept in and filled her up.

If she were honest with herself, she enjoyed King Asa's company. A lot. He was kind, gentle, and never pressured her. The night she'd spent with him, while a stimulating and tantalizing experience, had left her with conflicting thoughts.

She had promised her subjects Platirius would never be ruled by a king again, and she meant it. She wanted to hold onto the reins for as long as she could. She hoped in time, he'd understand.

"Would you like to stay for luncheon? I could whip up the bruschetta and some soup, and we can eat in the garden?"

"Nothing would make me happier. Lead the way."

Queen Dellah's statue smiled down on her daughter and her friend entering the palace.

"So there I was with a honey on the right and one on the left and no way of explaining why they were both there at the same time."

Dr. Clint shook his head. "I try to be a good MaleForm, Dr. Ascencio, but there are too many beautiful WomenForms out there for me to have just one."

Justin laughed. "When we're outside of work, call me Justin, please. So how did you get out of it?"

"I acted like I passed out."

"What?!"

"Yeah. I passed out right there in the club with both of them standing over me. I figured if they really loved me, they'd contact emergency services. Do you know what they did?"

"What?"

"They left me there and went shopping together!"

Justin double over with laughter.

Dr. Clint bit into his fish sandwich. "Wow, this is pretty good," said Dr. Clint. "It's not greasy and not fried too hard." Popping a couple of the crispy chips into his mouth, he said, "I think this is one we can put on the books as a winner."

Justin agreed. The smoked salmon platter and fried oysters with garlic mashed potatoes were delicious. A band he wasn't familiar with played on stage.

"The music is good too," he said.

Dr. Clint nodded toward the stage. "They have open mic night here every weekend. Beings get up there and sing or spout poetry. I've never been here in the daytime before today, but it's just as busy as the night crowd."

A pretty waitress with jet black butterfly locks and hazel eyes approached their table. "Would you like to order anything else? Or get a refill on your drinks?"

"I'll take another PeachBerry Fitz, please," said Dr. Clint.

"Another sweet PotterBerry juice for me, please," said Justin.

"Alright. Any dessert?" she asked.

They both declined.

She looked over at Justin as she refilled their drinks.

"I haven't seen you here before. I'm Toni. I hear you're a doctor at the Azini Institute."

He watched the deep burgundy liquid cover the ice in his glass.

"Is it true you're dating Dr. Azini?"

Justin sputtered, choking on his juice. He let out a series of coughs before he got himself under control.

Staring up at her, he said, "Excuse me?"

She shrugged. "Well, that's the rumor—that you and she are a couple."

"Well, the rumor is false," said Justin. "I don't date anyone I work with."

Toni eyed him suspiciously. "Then who did you order clothes for? My sister works at one of the boutiques and saw your order when it transmitted."

"Umm," said Justin. "I don't think that's any of you or your sister's business."

"JanIus is a tiny planet, Dr. Ascencio. We don't have silly things like gossiping decrees here like on Platirius. Everyone here knows everybody's business. You should get used to it."

"Well, maybe that's something I need to nip in the bud right now," said King Leighton, coming from behind her.

She broke into a sweat when the king stopped before her.

"I value privacy. I don't like hearing my Beings are invading each other's spaces."

Toni bowed to him. "I'm sorry, King Leighton."

"Show me how remorseful you are by keeping your nose out of others' business. No need to tell your sister, I'm sure word will get to her before the luncheon hour ends. I've never had to issue a gossip decree, but I think now is a good time."

He turned from Toni and elevated his voice so everyone could hear him. "I'll only say this once: Please mind your own business and work with your hands as you have been instructed to. That comes from the realm of The One, does it not?"

The silence that swept the place was deafening. Their king was easygoing, but some of his subjects had learned not to mistake his kindness for weakness.

"And just in case some of your memories are faulty, I'll have my team draft it and transmit it to you before the day ends. You're not to ask anyone about their personal business, nor are you permitted to spread unfounded rumors. Am I clear?"

After everyone answered the king, he nodded. "Very good. Now please return to your duties."

Justin was stunned. He hadn't seen this hardened side of the king before. He supposed he had to be firm and direct sometimes to maintain order and control. The music started up again. Without another glance at Justin, Toni hurried to take another order.

King Leighton smiled at Justin and Dr. Clint. "I hope you're enjoying the food. They have the best carrot and raisin slaw and carrot cake cookies I've ever tasted. I'm quite partial to carrots."

Dr. Clint raised his glass to the king. "I'll keep that in mind."

King Leighton met Justin's eyes. "I doubt you'll have any more issues after today, but if you do, please let me know and I'll take care of it. Immediately."

Noting the steel in the king's eyes, Justin nodded.

"Yes, Your Highness."

The king softly clapped his hands together. "Well, I'll let you get back to your lunch. I found a baby bird with its neck broken on my way in. I had the gardening staff dispose of it, but I'm curious how it happened. I haven't seen its mother around."

"Maybe it fell out of its nest and she didn't notice."

The king thought it was plausible, but for reasons he couldn't understand, his senses were on high alert.

"It's never happened here before. We don't have accidental deaths around here—be it Beings or creatures."

He looked up into the sky. Soft lavender clouds were closing in on the sun's rays, casting a dark shadow over the warm atmosphere.

"I've never liked surprises," said the king. "Life has taught me not all of them are pleasant."

Chapter 6

"Whoa there, Doc!"

Justin felt strong hands on each side guiding him off the grass and onto the paved road. An old MaleForm with an eyepatch and close-cropped white hair grinned up at him with perfect teeth. His weathered skin didn't match the youthfulness in his eye.

Pointing to a medium-sized hole, he said, "You almost stepped into that hole there. You would've twisted your ankle for sure." He pushed up a beaten-up old hat off his brow. "Then you would've needed doctoring!"

Justin looked at the hole and said, "Thank you. I didn't notice it. I don't think it was there yesterday."

"Well, you took a different route going home, so you wouldn't have seen it. That young gardener probably forgot about it before he went home."

Gallium doesn't strike me as careless, thought Justin.

The old MaleForm scratched his cheek. "The funny thing about holes is...sometimes we dig ourselves in so deep, we can't get out."

Before Justin could analyze his statement, he waved his hand and said, "Well, never mind. All that ends well, yeah? I'll go on and fill this up and let you get on with your day."

Justin nodded at him. "Thank you, mister— What's your name?"

Still grinning, he placed his hands on his hips. "Beeman! Just call me, Beeman."

"Alright. Have a good day, Beeman!"

"I will, Dr. Ascencio. I'll be seeing you soon."

A strange feeling fluttered in Justin, but Beeman pointed to his eye.

"It's been a long time since I was in the war, but this gets to bothering me sometimes. I'm hoping you can help me."

"Uh, sure. I'm not an ophthalmologist, but make an appointment and I'll see what I can do for you. If I can't help, I'll refer you to someone who can."

Beeman slapped his hands together. "That'll do it! Enjoy your day, Doc!"

"You too, Beeman."

A peculiar old fellow, thought Justin as he entered the building.

Beeman watched him until he was out of sight.

The atmosphere was busier than Justin had ever seen. Now that Fawn was in charge, Beings were pleased they didn't have to travel to other galaxies to receive medical care.

Although the WomenForms liked and trusted Fawn's leadership, Justin hadn't lost any of his patients—especially the females. Ms. Dill kept her promise and returned. She was the first patient waiting for him when he arrived.

He smiled warmly at her. "Well, Ms. Dill! I see you're back. What seems to be the issue this time?"

She watched him wash his hands before turning on the TransScreen.

"I'm going to have an InfantForm."

He pivoted sharply toward her. "Oh? Well, that's wonderful news! But I'm not a ParaNurture physician. You'll have to see Dr. Azini for treatment."

"No, it's not wonderful, and I don't want to see her. She'll probably try to talk me out of it." She grimaced. "There's nothing wrong with my *Annilose* levels, but I was so discombobulated, I forgot to activate it before his...fluid reached my eggs. By the time I realized I hadn't, it was too late! I was carrying." Her eyes filled with tears. "I don't want it inside of me."

He slowly lowered his body into his chair. "I don't want to pry into your private life, but I'm sure you came to see me for a reason."

She wrung her hands. "I trust you, Dr. Ascencio. I have no issue with Dr. Azini, but I won't go to her."

"Why not, Ms. Dill?"

"Her father is the reason I'm in this mess."

Fighting back tears, she said, "I bumped into him outside the institute after my appointment with you. He wanted to make conversation, but I blew him off and went home. The next thing I knew, he was standing at my door, pretending I'd forgotten something, but my memory is iron sharp."

He waited patiently until she was ready to continue.

"I knew I hadn't. When I asked him to leave, he barged into my home and forced himself on me. I might like to have fun, but he was never my type. I repeatedly told him no and to leave."

Her hand cinched around the collar of the thick medical gown. "That should've been enough. He got mad when I said he'd never be a better doctor than you." She burst into tears. "I shouldn't have said that! Maybe if I hadn't, he would've left me alone!"

He wanted to comfort her, but not wanting to make her feel worse, he refrained from touching her. She was grateful when he grabbed a couple of tissues and handed them to her.

"No. Don't ever think that. It wasn't your fault. It was his. There was nothing you could have said or done to make him assault you. Please don't blame yourself for his actions."

"I'm so stupid! How could I let this happen? What will everyone think when they find out? They'll blame me!"

She blew her nose. "I can't have this baby. I shouldn't be forced to have it!"

"Let me call Dr. Azini. I'm your doctor. I don't have
to disclose who the father is, and I won't. We're strict on
patient confidentiality—nothing you say goes further than here.
Alright?"

She sniffed. "Alright."

In less than five minutes, Fawn knocked on the door.

"Hello, everyone! Ms. Dill, Dr. Ascencio asked me to step in
here to help with something. What's going on?"

Justin listened as Ms. Dill told Fawn what she'd shared with
him, except the identity of the InfantForm's father.

"I see," said Fawn. "Well, in special circumstances such as this,
terminating the pregnancy wouldn't be against the rules. We
have to stick to the protocol. Dr. Ascencio isn't a ParaNurture
physician. He can't perform the procedure, but I can."

Ms. Dill wrapped her shawl around her shoulders when Fawn
sat next to her. "How soon can it be done?"

"We could have you scheduled within a week," said Fawn.

"I don't want anyone to know why I'm here," said Ms. Dill.

"Ms. Dill, I assure you, we keep the strictest security measures
here," said Fawn. "I'm sure Dr. Ascencio informed you that
patient confidentiality is our top priority. We'll schedule you for
surgery. There's no need to go into further detail than that."

Ms. Dill buried her nose into the tissue. "Good. Let's get it
over with then."

Fawn refrained from touching her hand. Respecting her
personal space was crucial. "After you've recovered from the

procedure, I'd like to schedule you for a consult with Dr. Barbara."

Ms. Dill quickly scooted away from Fawn. "No. I'm not crazy! No one is locking me away for something that wasn't my fault!"

"We don't lock up survivors of assault, Ms. Dill," said Justin. "You'd go to outpatient counseling and talk about what happened to you."

"I don't want to talk about it," said Ms. Dill. "I just want to get on with my life!"

Justin handed her more tissues when the tears began flowing down her face again.

"I want to be happy again!"

"Let us help you get there," said Justin. "We don't think you're crazy, and counseling is nothing to be ashamed of. I should know. I went when I was having a rough time getting bullied in med school. It helped."

Ms. Dill looked at him for a long time. "I'll think about it. Right now, I just want to get it over with. That's all I have energy for right now."

Fawn and Justin glanced at each other.

"Alright, Ms. Dill," she said, moving closer to the TranScreen. "I'll schedule you now. When can you return?"

"I can take leave from my job. I never report off, so I have plenty of time saved."

Fawn scheduled the appointment and handed her a lavender card with her name written in gold writing.

"Thank you for allowing us to help you. I'm so sorry for what happened to you, but please know we care," said Fawn.

Ms. Dill took the card and nodded. "Thank you both. Goodbye."

The doctors sat in silence for several moments.

"You know, I knew this would be a part of the job, but I don't think you're ever ready to hear stories like that," said Fawn.

"I think you handled it with grace and compassion. She was worried we'd judge her. I think it helped for her to know we're on her side."

"When I was a ChildForm, I wondered why the queens killed most of the MaleForms on Platirius. Now I understand. Some of the MaleForms here think WomenForms aren't worth the spit out of their mouths."

Justin sat back and crossed his legs, listening.

"We have some of the most despicable ones right here on our planet. What if JanIus did a cleanse? Just...got rid of all those who think like my father did?"

"I don't think King Leighton would go for that."

"Oh, I know he won't. Just wishful thinking, I guess."

"It's true, many of them are evil, but I thank The One we have more than a few good ones walking around. The king is less misogynistic than his father and wants to change things. I believe things will turn around in time."

"They might, but how many more WomenForms will have to suffer like Ms. Dill? What do we do until then?"

"We continue having the perpetrators arrested and standing before the justice council to face accountability. That's all we can do. I believe in JanIus's justice system. If someone goes before them, they deserve to be there."

She slapped her hands on her thighs. "I agree. We have more patients to see, Justin. Let's try to put this behind us for now."

She stretched and stood. "I'm going to run to the cafe on the corner and grab some chamomile tea. I need something relaxing after that. Do you want anything?"

"No, thank you. Thank you for helping her, Fawn. I mean it."

"That's what I'm here for. See you in a while!"

"In a while," said Justin.

"Dr. Ascencio, your next patient is a little spitfire," said a NurseForm as she passed him. "He refused to see anyone except you."

"Okay. It sounds like today will be a wild one."

He opened the door of the next examination room to find a special friend.

"Tautumn! What's up, little guy? I'm very happy to see you."

Tautumn peered around him suspiciously. "Are you by yourself today?"

Justin turned on the TranScreen. "Yes. Why? Is something wrong?"

The ChildForm shook his head. "No. I just didn't want to talk to anyone except you."

"Is everything alright at the Overmills' place?"

"Oh yeah. They're very nice Beings, but..."

Justin's brow furrowed. "But what?"

"The king said our father would be coming to get us soon, but he hasn't. Whenever I ask the Overmills about him, they keep changing the subject." Worry etched over his small face. "Did something bad happen? Have you heard anything about him?"

"No, I haven't, but I'll make it a priority to get answers for you. Alright?"

Tautumn nodded. "I didn't lie to come here. I cut myself playing basketball yesterday. Can you look at it?"

"Sure," said Justin. "Let's have a look."

The cut was small and not infected. Justin cleaned it with iodine and secured it with a bandage.

"I don't need to prescribe anything, so I'll have my NurseForm write a pass to excuse you from classes for the morning. But I expect you to return to your instruction chamber this afternoon. Do we have a deal?"

"Sure." Tautumn bit his lip. "Could you not tell the Overmills what you find out about my father?"

Justin's brow furrowed. "Why not? Are you unhappy with them?"

"No. I just feel they know more than what they're telling me and my brothers. They're a nice couple, Dr. Ascencio, but they're not our father. We should be with him."

The young ChildForm was wise beyond his years. He reminded Justin of when he was a boy. There was a time when he, too, had longed for his real parents.

"I agree. Come back in a couple of days. I should have something for you then, okay?"

Reaching into a deep, crystal bowl on his desk, he fished out over a dozen hard candies. "Here, share these with your brothers and tell them I said hello."

Tautumn quickly placed the candy in his backpack. "Will do, Dr. A! Thanks," he said running out of the chamber at full speed.

Justin called after him. "No running in the halls!"

Tautumn's pace slowed a bit, then sped up until he shot out the doors like a track star.

Justin chuckled. "When did you start sounding like an old fart, man?"

He washed his hands and prepared to see his next patient.

Fawn drained the last of her tea before tossing her cup into her recycling bin. She was down to her fourth patient and was looking forward to the luncheon hour.

She scanned her TranScreen and saw her next patient was a young MotherForm. She'd been assigned to Chamber 4. Just as she was about to rise from her desk, she heard a knock at the door.

"Come in," said Fawn.

"Hi, Dr. Azini," said Jonas, a mail staff. "This just arrived for you. It's a big sucker too!"

Fawn smiled and took the large package.

"I wonder what it could be?" asked Jonas, looking over her shoulder.

"I wonder who would ignore the king's decree about not minding the business of others?" said Fawn.

It worked. He flew out of her office faster than a TravelCraft. Fawn chuckled. She liked Jonas. All of the staff assigned to the institute got along well with each other. She was grateful for that.

Staring curiously at the package, she picked up a letter opener and carefully began removing the expensive paper. When she was finished, she gasped, staring at what she'd uncovered.

A life-sized painting of her father stared back at her. Noting his accusing eyes and haughty smirk, her hands shook furiously.

"Who could've sent this to me?"

Setting it down on the desk, she snatched up the card and read it. "I don't believe this! Of all the nerve!" she hissed.

Spinning on her heels, she hurried out of her office. A soft chime above Chamber 4 stopped her.

Damn!

It would have to wait. She had patients to see. She couldn't afford to keep them waiting. Knocking soundly on the door, she entered and pasted on what she hoped was a professional smile.

"Hello, Mrs. Zandi. I'm Dr. Azini. Nice to meet you."

She noticed the WomanForm had bags under her eyes, and her disheveled blouse and skirt were a size too large.

"How are you feeling?"

"Not too well, Dr. Azini. My baby cries all day and night. I haven't had any rest since she was born. I make sure she's fed and changed, but she still cries. My husband won't help me with her, and I don't know what to do."

For the first time, Fawn noticed a sleeping InfantForm next to her. After quickly washing and drying her hands, she peered down into the sleeping baby's face.

"She's beautiful!" Fawn gushed. "It's not uncommon for babies to forgo sleep when they're this young. You say she cries in the daylight too?"

The MotherForm shook her head miserably. "No matter what I do, she won't stop. I'm so tired. She won't let me eat or sleep. I haven't had a moment's peace until today." She glanced at the soft lilac wallpaper trimmed in deep plum. "I guess it's something about this chamber that calmed her down."

Mrs. Zandi peered into her baby's face. "Don't be fooled by this. She sleeps when we're in TravelCrafts, but the minute we get home, she's up and crying again."

Fawn smiled down at the baby. "I read her name is Kori. What a beautiful name. We'll check her out and see if we can determine the issue. If not, it could be colic."

Mrs. Zandi shot Fawn a concerned glance. "What's that?"

"It's excessive crying for long periods with no plausible reason. We might not determine the factor, but it could be an underdeveloped digestive system, food allergies, or anxiety caused by family stress."

Fawn pulled up a chair and sat down, crossing her legs. "I'm not blaming you or your husband. I just want to get a feel for how things are with your family. Are you two doing okay?"

"Well, he's happy to be a father, but he hates the crying. It keeps him up at night, and he needs to be alert for work."

Fawn nodded. "I understand. Any particular food allergies for you or him?"

"My husband is allergic to carrots, but I love them!"

Mrs. Zandi ducked her head. "I snuck a couple when she wouldn't stop crying. It might sound odd, but they calm me down. They always have."

Fawn noted it on the TranScreen. "I see. Do you breastfeed?"

"Yes," said Mrs. Zandi.

"Have you breastfed after you ate carrots?"

"Yes, but I didn't think anything was wrong with it."

"It may not be an issue," said Fawn, looking up from the TranScreen. "Let's get you both checked out. I don't want you to start feeling unwanted emotions. You look exhausted and sound guilty when you shouldn't. You're not to blame for her crying. I also want to refer you to see Dr. Barbara."

Mrs. Zandi rearranged the baby's tiny cap. "There's nothing wrong with my mind, Dr. Azini."

"Oh, no! I'm not saying that at all."

She paused to listen to Kori's heartbeat. "I understand you may be distrustful of seeing our mental wellness physician due to how mental health was handled in the past. But I assure you, we have good staff here committed to ensuring that our minds receive excellent care too. It's not enough to be physically healthy anymore. In these times, the mind is just as important as the body. Does that make sense?"

Mrs. Zandi shrugged. "I guess so. I won't be locked up away from my baby, right?"

"We don't lock anyone up at the institute unless they're a danger to themselves or others. Do you have any thoughts of harming yourself or the baby?"

"No, of course not."

"Okay. Then we'll get started. If it's an allergic reaction, we should be able to determine it before you leave today."

For the first time, Mrs. Zandi smiled. "Thank you, Dr. Azini."

Fawn smiled at her. "You're welcome. I'll be right back!"

Fawn had the results of Kori and her mother's bloodwork back within the hour.

"Alright, Mrs. Zandi, we found the culprit. I'm afraid you'll have to give up the carrots if you want a good night's rest. Baby Kori's tummy can't handle them."

Mrs. Zandi covered her mouth. "Oh no. So I was hurting her!"

Fawn laid a hand on her shoulder. "You didn't know. If you had, you would've stopped eating carrots. Now we're aware and no harm has been done."

She stroked the baby's hair. "She's perfectly healthy. You've been taking excellent care of her. As for you, I've prescribed some vitamins. You're underweight. Make sure you take one every day and continue eating a diet of fruit, vegetables, and lean meats. And toss in a couple of treats occasionally until you're back to your former size."

Tears of relief shone in Mrs. Zandi's eyes. "Thank you, Dr. Azini. It'll be good to finally get some rest."

"No need for thanks," said Fawn as she entered data into the system. "I'm scheduling you to return to see me in a month. You can check out at the counter. In a while, little Kori."

Her bright smile faded when she remembered the painting. She was determined to find out why it had been sent to her.

J ustin knocked soundly on Dr. Chirp's door.

"Oh, hello, Dr. Ascencio! What's going on?"

"I'm headed out to pick up lunch and wanted to get your order."

"Ooh! Thank you!" she said, switching from her work shoes to comfortable slippers.

"I'm craving some deep-dish pepperoni pizza and a salad!" She looked up at Justin. "Is the cherry cheese pie on the menu today?"

"They have mango cheese pie today."

"Oh, that sounds fabulous! I'd like a slice of that please and some sweet AppleBerry juice!"

"You got it."

She held up her palm and sent the payment to Justin's outstretched hand. He smiled down at the sum on his hand. Transmitting through palms was something he still hadn't become used to.

"Keep the change if there's any."

Justin shook his head. "No can do. But I'll buy another slice of cheese pie for you to keep in your ice box here for later."

Dr. Chirp smiled up at him. "You have a heart of gold, Dr. Ascencio!"

"Ah, my heart is full. Thank you."

He spotted one of her birds sitting on the counter. It was blue with a white head. Her brother fluttered up to a high window, focused on something below.

"And who do we have here?" he asked, moving closer to the bird. "Hello, little darling. How's your day been?"

She watched him approach her. When he reached out to touch her head, her mouth opened and—

"Ouch!" Justin shouted.

"Oh no! What happened?" asked Dr. Chirp, rushing over to them.

"She bit me!" said Justin. "She got me right between my thumb and pointer finger."

"No! Don't do that!" said Dr. Chirp.

She reached up and prevented him from sucking the bitten area. "It could get infected if your saliva is mixed with hers. Let me see."

Carefully, she washed the bite and placed antiseptic ointment on the wound.

Justin frowned at Mystery when she placed a tiny bandage on his hand. "She's not the friendliest soul, is she?" he muttered.

Dr. Chirp laughed. "I'm sorry. I should've warned you. Mystery isn't very friendly, but Cervantes is!"

Justin looked up at the male bird who continued staring out the window, ignoring them.

"I'll keep that in mind. I'd better get going. I have fifteen lunch orders to bring back. It'll take a while for the cafe staff to get them ready."

"Thank you for including me, Dr. Ascencio."

"Hey, we're all family here, right? I'd be an ass if I didn't. In a while, Dr. Chirp."

"In a while!" She looked over at Mystery, who was still glaring at Justin. "You're a mean little thing. He's one of the nicest MaleForms I've ever met. Try to be kind, okay?"

The bird cocked her head and let out a shrill whistle. "He's a hot piece!" she quoted.

Dr. Chirp gaped at her. "Mystery! Where did you hear that?"

"Well, it's good to see you again," said Justin.

Beeman turned around. "Oh, Dr. Ascencio. Is it luncheon already?"

"Yes, I'm here to pick up everyone's order. Have you eaten?"

Beeman's expression was unreadable. He shook his head.

"Nah. I forgot to add funding to my account. I won't be eating today. I often can't afford it, but it's nice to smell the food cooking."

"Well, I'll have some time after I submit the orders. Why don't you come in and have a bite? My treat."

"Why would you do that for a stranger?"

"Let's just say it's for saving me from falling on my ass today."

Beeman stared at him for a moment. "Alright. I've been smelling those chicken cylinders for a good hour. I can't turn them down."

Justin laughed. "Excellent. Let us go!"

Beeman looked down at the fried chicken cylinders, pasta with cheese, and stewed tomatoes and smiled. "They make the best chicken cylinders. I haven't had them since I was a ChildForm. In some places of the galaxy, no one knows how to prepare them."

Justin cocked his head. "Is that right?"

"Oh yes," said Beeman with a mouth full of chicken. "It's an old Coldarian recipe."

Justin's hand stilled. "You know of the Coldarians?"

Beeman shook his head. "They were before my time, but many of their recipes have been around for years."

He sampled a bite of the tomatoes. "I guess some things are hard to let go. And some Beings."

Justin wondered what he meant, but then Beeman said, "You're a wealthy doctor who's done good charity work today. Are you proud of yourself?"

Justin raised an eyebrow at the offhand comment. "I don't look at this as charity. As I said before, I'm happy to do it."

A half-smile was on Beeman's face. "I'm just joking. I have a dark sense of humor sometimes."

Justin focused on his old, gnarled hands. Something was off about Beeman, but he couldn't put his finger on it.

Beeman nodded his head toward the institute. "There's some beautiful WomenForms working there. You must be prying them off with a shovel. Having access to Sulphanite is convenient, huh? Then your treasure won't fall off."

He laughed harshly.

"I don't spread myself thin between females, nor do I soil where I eat," said Justin sternly.

"Well, I don't blame you for not bouncing them on your thighs two at a time, Doc. Plenty of Beings look good on the outside."

He looked squarely into Justin's eyes. "But they're as rotten as diseased cattle on the inside."

Justin felt a chill go through him. Beeman's personality was beginning to rub him the wrong way.

"I haven't detected any toxicity in my colleagues. As a matter of fact, I feel very blessed to work with them."

Beeman bit into the chicken without taking his eye off of him. "And what about that female leader? Dr. Azini's daughter? Is she a cold fish or not?"

What's with this guy? thought Justin. *Why is he so negative?*

"I have nothing but respect for Dr. Azini. She treats her patients and her staff with kindness and respect. She's a fine leader."

"You gotta admit, she fills out her pants quite nicely."

Justin thought he had the cruelest laughter he'd ever heard.

When he didn't join in, Beeman waved his hand and said, "You'll have to overlook me sometimes, Doc. I didn't grow up with the best mother. I learned to crack off jokes to deal with the pain of having a mother who wished I hadn't been born."

"I'm sorry about that, Beeman," said Justin.

"Well, we all can't have beautiful mothers who sit around, waiting to hear from us, can we?"

Justin winced.

Beeman nodded firmly. "Yes, I envy the poor souls who do."

Raising a glass, he said, "To the lucky ones, Doc. Amen, and may The One bless them!"

"Yes," said Justin. "I pray for every Being's blessing and protection."

"Hm. The One is a fickle character, Dr. Ascencio. He has His chosen ones He protects with His last breath. But sometimes He lets others take a nasty fall. Especially the bastards. Bastards have the hardest lives—until they die."

Chapter 7

Justin finished delivering all the lunch orders and sat down to enjoy his food when Fawn entered his office.

"Hey, are you coming to eat with me?"

"No. I lost my appetite when I found your little gift."

His eyebrows raised. "My gift? And what would that be?"

Her hands flew to her hips. "Why would you send a painting of my father to me?"

"Me? I wouldn't send something like that. I don't know anyone who likes your father enough to paint him and make it a gift."

He examined the card she showed him. "This is crazy! Fawn, I didn't send this. I argued with Dr. Azini just before I passed out. For all I know, he slipped me something before he left that day. He's the last Being I'd ever consider for art!"

The pent-up indignation flowed out of Fawn like hot air releasing from a balloon.

"Then I don't understand. Why would someone send it to me and sign the card with your name?"

He shrugged. "I have no clue, but I hope you believe me."

He glanced at the card again. "And I hope you burned it."

"Not yet. I want to examine it more and see if I can figure out where it came from."

"It didn't come from one of the galleries around here?"

She shook her head. "No. I've called everyone I can think of around JanIus and two of our neighboring planets. No one was commissioned to paint it."

Justin moved his fork around in the cilantro lime rice. "That means someone painted it and sent it to you directly."

Fawn braced her hands on his desk. "But why? Everyone knew how my father was. Why would someone want to paint him and gift it to me?"

"Maybe they wanted to get under your skin. Have you made any enemies lately?"

"I haven't made any enemies as far as I know."

Justin expelled a breath. "I say get rid of it and put it out of your mind. If someone is playing a game, they don't deserve your energy. Or it could be he had it painted before he died, and the artist decided to send it over."

Fawn adjusted her neck, trying to get a kink out of it. "That's plausible."

"How about you bring your lunch in here and we forget about old what's his name?"

She smiled at him. "Sounds like a plan! I'll be right back!"

Without meaning to, he observed the curves of her behind when she exited. Beeman's misogynistic comments came flooding back to him. He shook his head.

Beeman had admitted he'd had a hard life. Justin didn't expect him to act like a proper gentleman.

When Fawn entered again with her lunch, they talked about everything except the newest member of the cleaning staff. If they had, they would've realized Fawn hadn't hired him.

*C*ode RED in Chamber 6! Code RED in Chamber 6!

Everyone rushed down the hallway. A code red meant someone was dying.

"It's Colonel Burham!" cried a NurseForm.

Fawn, Justin, and Dr. Clint were the first to arrive. Justin noted the colonel's breathing was unsteady and he was sweating profusely. Quickly, he checked the monitors.

"I need 1500 units of Quorodine fast!"

"We're all out! The nightshift recorded we were out and ordered more, but it won't be here until this afternoon!" said a NurseForm while Fawn checked his vitals.

"That doesn't make any sense," said Justin. "I placed the order last week. When I retrieved some vitamin supplements, I saw it. It was fully stocked yesterday."

A NurseForm shook her head. "We checked three times, Dr. Ascencio. There's none in the stockroom."

"His tongue is turning purple," said Fawn as she removed the medical day gown from his damp chest. Seeing deep purple welts on his chest, she said, "He's having some sort of reaction to something! Pull up his medical history on the overhead TranScreen!"

"Aritzapam?" read Dr. Clint. "He's allergic to it! Why was he prescribed that?"

"That's impossible," said Justin. "This is my patient! I ordered for him to be given 750 units of Lyzapham every two hours."

Fawn checked the TranScreen again. "He was given Aritzapam, not Lyzapham. That's why he's in distress. We can use Aricoshaltz to reverse the effects, but I need it now!"

"Yes, Dr. Azini!" said a NurseForm.

The colonel's chest heaved when Fawn administered the drug intravenously. She held her breath as the monitors continued sounding loudly. It was now or never. If it didn't work in the next couple of minutes, they'd lose him.

Everyone waited. Dr. Chirp took his hand and squeezed it for support. He was the oldest and most beloved soldier in the galaxy. No one wanted to lose him. Finally, the monitors began chiming normally, assuring the danger had passed.

Fawn sighed with relief. "Who gave the order for Aritzapam?"

Dr. Clint pulled up another screen and swallowed hard. "It says you did, Dr. Ascencio."

Justin's mouth dropped under the lavender mask. "There's no way in hell I did!"

Dr. Clint pointed to the screen. "Your signature is right here in black and white."

Justin looked at his palm. "But my order is here! It clearly says Lyzapham!"

A NurseForm wiped a bit of sweat from Fawn's brow. "Did you convert it to the TranScreen orders?"

"Of course I did! I entered it myself! I've been using this system for nearly two years. I'd never make an error like that!"

Justin surveyed the sad expressions of his colleagues.

They don't believe me!

"We have it under control now. Let's get the colonel comfortable again. Dr. Ascencio, I need to see you in my office after we finish up here."

A lump formed in Justin's throat. He hadn't meant to sound arrogant, but it was true. In all the years he'd been a doctor, he hadn't made a mistake.

He understood perfection was an illusion, but he'd never be so careless as to prescribe something that could've taken a life.

F awn and Justin sat at her desk with two steaming cups of orange and ginger tea.

"I've worked with you for a long time, so I know you're competent. But even you have to admit mistakes are unavoidable."

Justin shook his head. "Not like that. Not with my original order still on my palm."

"But you didn't use the scanner to transmit it into the system. You said you manually entered the data. That's why the scanning system is in place, Justin—to minimize the chances of prescription errors. Why didn't you use it?"

"I don't know," he admitted. "I didn't think about it, I just entered it. I do that often, and there's never been an issue."

"Until now. We had a big issue today and it's not something I can overlook."

She sighed. "I have to note this in your personnel file."

Justin set the cup down. "What? If you do that, I'll be on alert for a year! Two more mistakes and I won't be able to practice anywhere. Listen, just give me time to find out what happened."

She cocked her head. "And how will you do that? Our system is foolproof. I don't like admitting it, but my father built it to be flawless, and it is. I understand you don't like hearing you made a mistake, but if it were any of the other doctors, I'd make the same call. I can't afford to show favoritism, Justin, I'm sorry."

"I'm not asking for favoritism! I'm asking you to believe me when I tell you I didn't do it!"

"Like I believed you about the painting?"

Justin groaned. "So we're back to that?"

Fawn nursed the cup in her hands. "I don't believe you sent the painting, but I do believe you made an error with the colonel's meds. You didn't mean to, but it is what it is. I can't let it go, I'm sorry. Your disciplinary notice will be in the system by the end of the day. I expect you to sign it—with your palm—and follow up with me if you have any questions."

Justin nodded. "Alright. I don't like it, but there's nothing I can do about it." His fist tightened into a ball. "And I hate it."

"So do I," admitted Fawn. "But I have to be fair across the board."

"I know," said Justin.

Fawn nodded at him sadly.

After he left, she sat alone in her office, reflecting on the short time she'd led the institute. Until recently, things had been going smoothly. Now, strange events were happening without warning. She prayed today's catastrophe would be the end of it.

She wanted her practice to hold the number one spot—that included outranking Platirius and Revani's medical systems. However, if things continued, it would only be a figment of her imagination.

"You look depressed," said Gallium. "Cookie?"

Handing Justin a large lavender butter cookie, he sat down next to him.

Gallium surveyed the acres of beautiful landscaping with pride. JanIus was finally starting to look as attractive as the other planets.

"Why are you outside with the rest of us common Beings?"

"There was a medication error with a patient today," said Justin miserably. "I didn't do it, Gallium. I know I didn't."

"Who's the patient?" asked Gallium.

"I can't tell you that. Patient confidentiality."

Gallium grinned. "I know that. You're an ethical MaleForm, Prince Justin. You take after your grandfather, Carlomon."

He eyed Justin. "Have you had any more dreams?"

"Not a one. I guess I've been too stressed out lately to sleep well."

Gallium bit into the cookie and chewed. "What's bothering you?"

"I honestly don't know. Everything has been great, but now, things are happening I can't explain. It gives me an uneasy feeling."

"Everyone makes mistakes. Don't get into the habit of striving for perfection. It doesn't exist."

Justin craned his head to look across the courtyard. "Yeah, like that hole you left over there a couple months ago? If it weren't for a cleaning staff, I would've stepped in it and twisted my ankle! I guess if someone as skilled as you can make mistakes, maybe I need to consider I'm not as flawless as I thought."

Gallium scoffed. "What hole? Show me right now."

"Where do you get the bossiness from? You bark orders like a general!"

Gallium assessed him. "I *am* a general. I was appointed by your grandmother a long time ago."

Justin gawked at him. "You're a general, but you work for my mother?" He sat back in disbelief. "You could be running your own planet—be a king!"

Gallium looked down at his toes. "I've never wanted that."

"Why?"

"The same reason you don't want to be king. I love what I do. Now, are you going to show me the hole or not?"

Justin got up and led him to the spot where he'd seen the hole. Pointing, he said, "It was there. See how that mound doesn't quite match up with the others?"

As Gallium stared at it, Justin thought he felt the Coldarian's anger rise.

"That's not my work. I'd never leave something like that unattended."

He pointed to the sprouting purple lemon trees. "Every spot you see has fruit coming except that one. You say you were walking along and discovered it?"

"No. Beeman stopped me from stepping into it."

Gallium looked at him quizzically. "Who is Beeman?"

"He's a new cleaning staff. He looks old, which is odd. I don't see a lot of elderly Beings walking around JanIus."

Justin rubbed a hint of stubble on his chin. "To be honest, he's the only elder here."

Gallium's scalp prickled. "There aren't many, unless they practice sorcery. Manipulating time and space ages them. It's a punishment for meddling with The One's affairs. They're Satan's subjects. It's best to avoid them."

"Beeman doesn't seem like he practices magic," said Justin.

"How would you know? What do you know about sorcerers?"

"Nothing," admitted Justin.

Gallium's steady gaze was confident. "I know all about them. My gut tells me you should stay away from this Beeman character. I don't know why, but I get the feeling he dug that hole."

"But why? It doesn't make any sense, Gallium."

"I don't know, but I'll find out."

He looked up at the sky. "All the time I've been working here, it's been peaceful. The plants have been happy. But lately, I've felt a shift in things. I can't explain it, but it happened a few months before Coldarius exploded."

Gallium rubbed the top of his head. "I gave a SoloQuelle flower to my mother and told her to be careful. I failed her. I felt something was wrong, but I ignored my instincts. This time I won't."

Then maybe I didn't make a mistake with the colonel.

"I don't think you did," said Gallium.

Justin looked at him in wonderment. "You can read my mind?"

Gallium nodded once. "Yes. You're part Coldarian. But you can't read mine. You're not skilled enough."

Justin gazed at him thoughtfully. Something told him he didn't want to journey into Gallium's mind. Not ever.

"I have to get back now. I'll see you around."

"In a while, Prince Justin."

"Could you not call me that? I don't know who might be listening."

Gallium smiled wryly. "Last year, I would've said you were being paranoid. Now, I think you're on point. You be careful. I'll be watching."

After Justin raised his hand and left, Gallium's attention re-focused on the small, misshapen mound. Whoever made it had hastily covered it up, not caring about the precious soil smattered on the grass. He suspected it was Beeman. He used his power to even out the ground, leaving no sign it had ever been disturbed.

"If you were looking for trouble, you've found it."

Fawn met him at the door. "I didn't think you were coming back," she said.

"What do you mean?"

"Luncheon break is an hour. But the system says you signed out for two."

"That's not possible. I haven't been gone that long."

She pointed up at the timekeeper. "Yes, you have. Now, I don't mind if you need extra time as long as we're not busy. And due to what happened today, I'm willing to overlook it this time. Just talk to me if you're dealing with something." She patted him on the arm. "You're my colleague, but I also consider you a friend. You've always followed the rules. Let's keep that momentum going, okay?"

Justin's eyes sought the timekeeper when she walked away.

What on JanIus is going on?

"Hi, love. I expected you an hour ago. Is something wrong?"

"The craft stalled," said General Lyric miserably. "I can't get it to move. It crashed just outside of JanIus."

The nightmare of General Iham crashing into the water came hurtling back. He gripped the TeleScreen so hard, his knuckles turned white.

"Crashed? What do you mean crashed? Are you hurt?"

"No, but it's getting kind of spooky out here. Can you come and get me?"

"Say less, baby. I'm coming!"

General Lyric was elated to see the TravelCraft shooting toward her. She exploded from the craft, running full speed toward him. He picked her up and spun her around as if she weighed no more than a feather.

"Whoa," she said. "I'm not used to getting swung around!"

He kissed her soundly. "Well, get used to it, because I plan on doing it until I'm old and brittle."

"We don't age like that here, but I'm holding you to that, Your Highness. The queen is sending staff to take it back to Platirius, so you'll have to take me home."

"Good. That gives us more time to spend with each other," said Justin, embracing her again. "By The One, I've missed you."

His clean, fresh scent soothed her frayed nerves. "Your galactic speech is improving. I love it! Could you show me how much you missed me when we're on JanIus? I'm hungry!"

Justin seated the general at the table before taking his seat beside her. She surveyed the crowd before shifting her position.

"What's this? You don't want to be close to me?"

"Of course I do. I just don't like sitting with my back toward the door. It's easier to be ambushed."

Justin moved closer to her. "You're a born soldier, you know that?"

She smiled. "I wanted to make my father proud. Wherever he is, I hope I've succeeded."

General Iham's worried face shimmered in Justin's mind.

"I think he's very proud of his daughter. It's impossible not to be."

She squeezed his hand and picked up a menu. "I'm looking forward to eating this great food you keep telling me about."

"I've visited a lot of the night cafes around here, but this one is my favorite! You'll see why after you've eaten."

A waitress appeared to take their orders.

"You go first, Justin. I'm still looking."

"Alright. I'll have the salmon croquettes, grits with jalapeño and cheese, mojo pork, moros y cristianos, carne con papas, and a Cuban expresso, please."

"Ah, your Latin roots are showing," said General.Lyric.

He sighed. "I miss Cuba. I'd love to take you there one day. Have you ever been to Earth?"

"No. The queen hasn't assigned anyone there since she was appointed as Protector. She said we've learned enough about the Humans over the years and is content with allowing them to live as they please."

He didn't bat an eyelash at her order.

"I'll have two racks of beef ribs with sweet honey grilling sauce on the side, double orders of baked cheese pasta and sour cream and chive mashed potatoes, and a single order of carrot slaw. I'll also take a mug of sweet PeachBerry juice and peach scone pudding, please."

"Whoa there, you eat like two grown MaleForms, little lady. Watch out or you'll get as wide as a WarCraft!"

Beeman.

After the events of the day, Justin's patience was non-existent.

"There's nothing wrong with how much she eats, Beeman. You should mind your business."

Beeman held up a hand in surrender. "Hey, I'm sorry, pretty miss! Calm down, young JanIan. I meant no harm to the lovely lady. My tongue is a bit sharp sometimes."

"Then trim it," snapped Justin.

The general's hand went to his. "Justin. It's okay. He apologized."

Beeman smiled inwardly at the tension in Justin's shoulders.

General Lyric gestured to the open seat in front of them. "Won't you have a seat, mister? I don't believe we've met. I'm General Lyric."

Instead of shaking hands, Beings nodded in greeting. Using palms with strangers could result in data being mistakenly transmitted.

"Oh, I've heard of you! Who hasn't heard of the legendary General Lyric—one of the first WomanForms to be appointed general along with that other one. What's her name? The one with the big DingoPops?"

General Lyric stared at Beeman. "General Legend," she said evenly.

Although she and General Legend were hardly friends, she didn't appreciate how MaleForms referred to the shape of her body before they talked about her skills as a warrior. It was disrespectful to disregard her competence as a fighter.

"Will you be ordering supper?" she asked.

Beeman waved his hand. "Oh, no, no. I just came to say hello to the doc before heading home. I live in one of the old military chambers outside the palace. I'm hoping to save up to get one of those cottages by the institute."

"So you're not from JanIus?" asked Justin. "You'll be applying for citizenship then?"

Beeman nodded. "I hope so. I really like it here. It's perfect for an old soul to settle his bones."

Justin remembered Gallium's warning. "Where did you live before, Beeman?"

"Oh, all over," said Beeman dismissively. "I've never had a real home. Once I signed up for the military, we traveled everywhere. It's hard to find roots when you're a bastard."

He looked right into Justin's eyes and said, "Bastards aren't welcome in the galaxy, you know?"

Justin and General Lyric shared a look.

"I doubt King Leighton cares about familial pedigree. There are many Beings here that migrate from other worlds. What's important is following the rules and abiding by his decrees."

Beeman laughed. "Yes, King Leighton! He's so pretty, I swear he looks like a WomanForm!"

He laughed harder as Justin and the general stared at him.

"I'm just jesting. He is pretty for a MaleForm though. Pretty ones can be soft on law and order sometimes. Before you know it, he'll be opening up his borders to the Humans like that other king wanted to do."

Justin felt a familiar fluttering in his stomach.

Beeman stroked his sparse gray beard. "What was his name? Ah! King Carlomon! His heart was just as soft as his brain for wanting to let Humans into the galaxy."

His eye traveled from Justin's tight face to the general's bewildered one.

"You're too young to know about him. He passed when I was a baby, but the stories of his idiocy still live on."

General Lyric noticed Justin's hands had balled into fists under the table. Her hand swiftly went to his and closed over it, willing him to calm down.

"I've been told Humans have a very distinctive smell," said Beeman. "They smell like space hyenas. I hope I never come across one. I might have a bad flashback and kill it dead!"

The waitress arrived with their food, interrupting Beeman's quiet tirade.

"Here we go!" she said brightly. "Can I get you anything else?"

"No, thank you. We're good," said General Lyric.

Feeling a strange tension rise in the air, she nodded and scurried away.

"Oh, don't mind me, you two. I have a bit of a violent streak from my mother. She got a kick out of beating me before suppertime so she wouldn't have to feed me."

He looked at General Lyric. "I hope you had a better mother than I did."

She fingered the silver necklace around her neck. "I don't remember a lot about her. I know she was pretty and traveled a lot."

Beeman grinned at her. "Traveled?"

He caught sight of the necklace and went pale. Justin and General Lyric watched beads of sweat appear on his forehead. His old, wrinkled hands trembled violently.

"Beeman?" asked General Lyric. "Are you alright?"

Beeman licked his lips and shivered. "I—I don't feel so good."

Justin started to rise. "Let's get you over to the institute."

"No!" said Beeman sharply, holding up a pleading hand. "I'll be alright." His gaze traveled to the necklace again. "I just gotta get out of here!" He shot up and ran out of the café without another word.

General Lyric's eyes widened in shock. "What in the devil got into him?"

Bewildered, Justin watched him flee into the night. "I don't know, but it looks as if the hounds of hell are chasing him."

Beeman ran until he reached the edge of the institute and vomited. He retched until his stomach emptied. Placing a cheek against the cool surface of the building, he trembled.

"She's a Coldarian! But how? There's power inside that necklace! A great and terrible power!"

His eyes narrowed. "I'll fix you, General Lyric. I'm gonna take good care of you!"

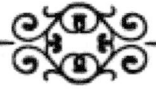

J ustin and Lyric made love twice before they fell asleep in each other's arms. Since time was precious, both wanted to put the strange encounter with Beeman behind them.

King Leighton's decree had eased their fears about Justin's identity being discovered, and they spent the entire weekend traveling and eating at various spots. He wiped her tears at the end of a sad movie.

Neither wanted their time to end. When it did, the familiar melancholy crept up and held onto them. She started packing up the last of her belongings after he went to start up the craft.

"Now where on JanIus is my perfume?"

It was her latest treasure. She was thrilled when he had surprised her with it. She couldn't leave it behind. Kneeling to look under the bed, she smiled. There it was. Right next to— Swiping her hand under the bed, she grabbed a soft, lacy pink bra that was two sizes too large for her and matching panties. Blood rushed to her face.

"These aren't mine," she muttered.

Justin noted she had little to say as they made the trip back to Platirius.

"I can't set foot on the grounds, Lyric. I got lucky last time, but you've seen what happens when I do."

"Yes, you become selfish and pig-headed."

He stared at her. "Yeah, that's one way to put it, I guess. Are you going to kiss me good-bye?"

Her tone was cold. "Never say good-bye. It's poor manners."

He grinned and pinched her thigh. "Alright, well kiss me until next time then."

The quick peck she planted on his cheek held less warmth than the ice cream they'd shared for dessert. When she left without saying a word, he sat dumbfounded. They'd had a wonderful time. He couldn't figure out why she'd turned so cold.

What did I do this time? he wondered.

Chapter 8

It was so silent, you could hear a pin drop when he entered. Dr. Chirp was crying and wringing her hands while Dr. Barbara patted her back solemnly. Dr. Clint was gazing out a window as if he were lost.

"What happened?" asked Justin.

"Oh, Dr. Ascencio," sobbed Dr. Chirp. "Dr. Azini is beside herself. She was performing the procedure expertly. Everything was going so well, and then..."

"And then what?" asked Justin.

"She—she died. The patient just died."

"Who? Who is 'she'?"

Dr. Chirp burst into a fresh round of tears.

Dr. Barbara said, "Ms. Dill. She started bleeding heavily."

Her lips trembled slightly. "We couldn't stop the bleeding. She died about twenty minutes ago. We did everything we could to save her, but we lost her. The InfantForm too."

H e found Fawn sitting in her office in the dark, her hands hanging limply at her side. Kneeling in front of her, he said, "Fawn? Fawn, look at me. I heard what happened. I'm so sorry."

Fawn's face was streaked with tears. "I don't know what went wrong. I meticulously planned the operation. There was no room for error."

He wrapped his strong arms around her. "Do you remember what you said to me after the colonel went into shock? Even the best of us make mistakes sometimes. That might not be the case this time. Maybe it was her time to go. When The One calls us, there's nothing we can do except answer."

Fawn sobbed into his shoulder. "I know. I know Death is always around the corner. But she trusted me, Justin. And I—I let her down."

"You didn't," he said fiercely. "You're an excellent doctor. You did your best. What more could you have done?"

She sniffed. "The queens trusted me too. They provided the program to save WomenForms, not have them die."

"Listen to me. The queens may be powerful, but they're Beings just like the rest of us. They're not higher than The One. No Being is. I'm confident everything went well with the procedure. It's just bad luck is all."

"Luck had nothing to do with it," said Dr. Corning as he entered Fawn's office with two soldiers. "It was something bad, alright. Something that should have never been in this institute."

Fawn lifted her head and looked at Dr. Corning.

"We got the results of her bloodwork back," said Dr. Corning. "Callidut was found in her system."

Fawn and Justin gasped.

"What?" cried Fawn.

"Yes, and that's not all."

His eyes shifted to Justin. "We received an anonymous tip you've been dealing Callidut out of here, Dr. Ascencio. I didn't want to believe it, but I had to notify King Leighton. Your office was searched and—we found dozens of vials of it. It's the same formula we found in her system."

"That's insane!" roared Justin. "I've never had my hands on any Callidut since I came here!"

One of the soldiers stepped forward. "Are you saying it's been in your possession before?"

Fawn's head whipped up to look at Justin, who immediately fell silent.

The soldiers seized both of Justin's arms. "Dr. Ascencio, you're under arrest for drug trading and murder. It would be in your best interest to come with us quietly."

Justin stood still while laser chains were wrapped around his wrists. As Fawn observed him get marched out of the institute, Beeman watched from a distance and smiled.

P rincess Teenah came running into the garden. "Mother! Mother, Prince Justin has been arrested on JanIus! It's all over the media!"

Queen Vivant dropped a handful of cucumbers into a basket. "What?!"

"W HAT DID YOU JUST *%$#@! SAY TO ME, LEIGHTON??" roared Queen Revari.

"We found Callidut in his office. I had no choice but to have him arrested. Drug trading goes against our strictest code."

Glaring at him, she pressed her face into the TranScreen. "Your guards placed their filthy hands on MY SON?! You idiot! Callidut is on MY realm. Gallium is the only one who makes it! It doesn't leave Revani without my permission! Release my son immediately."

"I can't do that," said King Leighton.

Queen Revari's eyes changed from silver to bright red. "Are you defying me?"

"If I let him go before he goes in front of the justice council, Beings will get suspicious. You ordered me to keep his identity a secret and I have."

General Legend rubbed the queen's shoulders to calm her down.

"But if anyone suspects I'm protecting him or showing favor, they might start digging into his past. I won't be able to protect him if the other kings come for him. And...he almost admitted he's had access to Callidut before."

General Legend placed her palm on her cheek. "He didn't say he tried to drug anyone with it, did he?"

"No, he stopped talking just in time, but my soldiers caught on."

If looks could kill, JanIus would've been absorbed into Revani.

"I have no choice, My Queen, I have to let him go before the council."

Gallium stood next to the queen. "I take it you have the Callidut in your possession?"

"Yes, of course."

"Don't turn all of it over to the justice council. Send it here so I can examine it. Wherever it came from, it isn't mine. Too many odd things have been happening on JanIus lately. Someone is trying to set the prince up."

"You know what this means, don't you, Leighton?" asked Queen Revari. "That greedy instructor thought she could cheat me by swindling funds from Vivant and I when Vivant had already paid her. I took care of her. I thought you were smarter."

King Leighton swallowed. "I never meant to fail you, Your Highness."

"Gallium and I will be there within the hour. No harm had better come to my son, or so help me, I'll send you to The One myself."

She disconnected the transmission. General Legend rushed to her side.

"My Queen, please listen to me. You can't go to JanIus!"

Queen Revari whipped her head around. "Are you insane, Legend? They have my son!"

General Legend kept her voice low and steady. "Yes, and if you go there, everyone in the galaxy will know it. They'll find out he's half-Human. You don't want that to happen, right?"

"You expect me to just sit by while my son is locked away like an animal?"

"No, My Queen," said Gallium. "But Legend is right. If you lose your temper, things could go badly for the prince."

She jumped out of her chair. "I'll behead everyone on that goddamn island! No one will hurt my son!"

Colonels Angela and Sheila rushed through the doors with Sergeant Kiana.

"What's going on?" asked Colonel Sheila. "Who are we killing today, My Queen?"

"Everyone, Colonel. Everyone who had a hand in hurting my son."

Colonel Sheila ran her thumb over her sword in anticipation.

Gallium took the queen by the arms and gently sat her down. "Please listen to me. Please? Let Legend and I go to him. You know the Callidut isn't ours. Justin told me about some Beeman character. He's been on my radar for a while now."

The queen's eyes narrowed. "Who is this Beeman?"

"He looks like an old MaleForm," said Gallium. "But I suspect it's a disguise or black magic has aged him. I've been following him for weeks but haven't found anything to nail him on. I know he reacted strangely to General Lyric one night."

Queen Revari scowled. "General Lyric? What does she have to do with this?"

"I don't know, but something made him run away from her and fast. I didn't come home until he bunked for the night."

Looking into her reddened eyes, he said, "Please, Queen Revari. Legend and I will protect Prince Justin with our lives. You know this."

"I'm his mother," she said. "I should be there for him."

"We can't risk someone finding out he's half Human."

"What if this Beeman already knows? Then what?" asked Queen Revari.

"Either way, we're gonna deal with him."

The deadly promise in Gallium's tone soothed her a bit.

"What will he think if I'm not there to comfort him?"

General Legend placed a hand on her shoulder. "We'll explain things to him. He knows you love him."

A bulletin appeared on the TranScreen.

A prestigious doctor was arrested on JanIus for murder. Bond is set at—

Sergeant Kiana nearly fainted at the amount.

Queen Revari pointed at her. "Get it ready for transmission to JanIus."

"Yes, Your Highness," said Sergeant Kiana.

"Stand down, Sergeant Kiana," said Queen Vivant.

Queen Revari whirled around to face her. "What are you doing here? Did you forget what planet you're on, sister? This is my realm. I give the orders here."

"I understand. I also understand my nephew is being unlawfully held on JanIus. I heard what Gallium and General Legend said, and I agree. Your temper is a hindrance. A cool head is needed for this job."

"This isn't your business, Vivant," hissed Queen Revari.

"Oh, but it is. I have just as much of a stake in JanIus as you. If you go in there without a plan, all of our investments will be lost. Let me go to Prince Justin. I'll make sure he's freed."

Queen Revari scrutinized her tailored navy suit with a platinum, satin tank underneath. Eight-inch navy heels and a navy fedora with tall, platinum feathers made a striking ensemble. She recognized the platinum and diamond necklace and bracelet circling her neck and wrist—they had belonged to their mother.

Dressed for a different kind of war, her beauty would disarm justice counselors on any planet. Pride swelled in Queen Revari before a spark of distrust snuffed it out like a puff of smoke.

"Why would you want to help my son after what he did to you? What's in it for you?"

Queen Vivant met her gaze steadily. "Maybe I'm making up for lost time. I didn't help him when he was a baby. Couldn't help him. But I can now. Please allow me, Revari. I won't fail you."

The queens silently assessed each other for a moment. "Do you swear no harm will come to my ChildForm?"

"I'll defend him with my life. On our mother's honor."

T he soldiers escorted Justin inside a confinement chamber and removed the laser restraints.

"I know this isn't what you're used to, but get comfortable," said Captain Josin. "You're not going anywhere for a while."

He looked Justin up and down. "I knew you were trouble the first time I laid eyes on you. Our king gave you a chance, and how did you repay him? You spit on his generosity. I hope he makes an example out of you."

Justin kept silent. What good would it have done to try to convince them he was innocent? No one believed him, not even his friends. That's what hurt the most. He'd never been incarcerated before. Never. He gazed at the smooth finish of the walls and the spotless floor.

To his left was a fancy bed, padded with plush cushioning and plump pillows. A deep plum comforter and pillowcases made it look inviting. Next to it was a tall bookcase filled with dozens of books, and on the other side of the wall was a large TranScreen. If he wanted to watch a specific program, his choices were transmitted from his palm to the screen.

On his right was a small bath chamber, complete with expensive toiletries. A small table in sat in the center of the room. To him, it looked like a five-star hotel room, not prison.

He sighed as he sank into the bed's firmness. It wasn't too soft or too hard. He could sleep if he wanted. After all of the terrible things that had happened to him, he should've been wound-up, but he wasn't. He lay down on the mattress and soon drifted off to sleep.

Justin and King Carlomon stood on the edge of a cliff high above the waves crashing below.

"Where are we, Great-Grandfather?"

"We're in a realm between the living and the dead. When your spirit is weakened, The One's power is stronger. As His messenger, I've come to tell you what you must do. The CarogueStone was gifted to me by my father. I wore half of it around my neck, and gave the other half to my first love. It had no power when I was a young soldier, but once I became king, the essence of Coldarius was ingrained into it. She refused to return the other half to me and split it between her daughters."

King Carlomon turned from the raging waters to face Justin. "King Dubian stole mine when he murdered me. When Coldarius exploded just before it was absorbed into Platirius, the CarogueStone became cursed by Platirius's dark magic. It shattered into smaller pieces. One of the shards flew into a small, abandoned planet. It slowly changed from red to a deep violet. Soon, life began to multiply on it."

"JanIus!" exclaimed Justin. "JanIus was made from a piece of the CarogueStone!"

"Yes. JanIus is Coldarius's future. It must be protected. Another part of the stone is in the center of the Earth, perched at the door of hell. My granddaughter sold another piece to a Platzarian prince."

He turned to Justin. You must find all the pieces and reunite the CarogueStone. Then say, If The One wills it, enter the king."

"But why? Enter from where?"

King Carlomon's eyes had been murky the first time Justin saw him. Now they were clear orbs of sparkling emerald. "I'm not permitted to tell you. The CarogueStone is the only way to save the galaxy. If you fail, all will be lost. No Being should be powerful enough to control all the realms. It's against the rules."

"How can I do anything when I'm trapped in here?"

A mysterious twinkle nestled in the king's eyes. "Only a king can set another king free. Since you're the last MaleForm descendant of my bloodline, the task falls to you."

"I'd have to take a planet," said Justin.

"Yes. A life for a life. A crown for a crown."

Justin's shoulders sagged. "I've never killed anyone in my life. There has to be another way!"

King Carlomon observed him. "It's the only way. I must go now. Look for me among the stars when you sound the horn."

"What horn?" asked Justin.

He watched him enter the starry sky of Space. His shadow disappeared when the moon's light hid him from the realms of the living. He blinked and found himself behind Gallium. Gallium's hand journeyed to the center of JanIus and grabbed the stone.

The soft chime of the timekeeper jolted him awake. He sat up on the side of the bed, allowing the remnants of the dream to slowly fade.

The CarogueStone is scattered around the galaxy. I can't put it back together unless I become king. How in the world will I do that?

He sighed, running his fingers through his hair.

My BrainStaff! It has to have the answers! Damn! I left it at the institute.

Doubting that anyone would bring it to him, he lay back on the bed in a huff. "I can't solve any mysteries in here. And that's exactly what someone wanted!"

D r. Chirp held out Justin's backpack to Fawn. "I took it out of his office before the soldiers trashed it. He's innocent, Dr. Azini! Justin would never do something like that!"

Fawn retrieved the backpack from her. "I know. I feel it in my bones. Terrible things have been happening for months."

Dr. Clint rapped his knuckles on the smooth surface of the conference table. "Someone is setting Justin up to take a fall!"

"I agree," said Dr. Barbara. "We all know him well enough to know his character."

"Now wait a minute," said Dr. Corning. "Last year, I found him passed out in his office. When he finally came to, he was rambling about seeing Beings inside walls. Now if that isn't a sign he's addicted to something, then you tell me what is!"

"I think it's a sign he had a medical emergency and needed help. If you remember, he was in a coma. Were drugs found in his system?"

Dr. Corning faltered. "Uh... Well, no. We didn't find anything abnormal."

Fawn got in his space. "So how do you determine he was on drugs?"

He stared at the table while everyone waited for him to respond.

Fawn continued staring him down as if he were the one who was carted away to a confinement chamber.

"At this institute, we don't wrongfully accuse our colleagues without definite proof. I hope if one of us passes out, you'll assist us instead of jumping to conclusions!"

He winced under her scathing tone. "I apologize to everyone. It was unfair for me to make baseless assumptions."

Nervously pushing his glasses up on his nose, he said, "Until recently, Justin's work has been impeccable. We owe it to him to be fair and impartial."

Fawn nodded firmly. "I agree. Thank you, Dr. Corning. Now, how are we going to prove Justin is innocent?"

"D r. Justin Ascencio, you've been charged with drug trading and the murder of two Beings. How do you plead?"

"Not guilty, Madame Justice Counselor," said Justin.

Justice Counselor Ava Gabari peered at the notes on the TranScreen before looking up at Justin.

"It says here over fifty vials of Callidut were found in your office. How do you explain that?"

"I would advise the doctor to be silent," said a voice.

Justice Counselor Gabari looked up. "Who dares to interrupt this council? Show yourself or face being in contempt of this court!"

A short WomanForm stepped forward. "I'm Defense Counselor Geena Harlowe. I'm representing Dr. Ascencio."

The justice counselor peered behind her. "And who is that standing behind you?"

The tall figure stepped forward.

"Queen Vivant?"

Thrown off guard by the queen's grand entrance, everyone in the justice chamber was speechless. The justice counselor searched the faces of her colleagues. The six male members stood, staring in awe at the queen.

"What brings you to JanIus, Your Highness?"

"I've brought legal counsel for Dr. Ascencio, and I'm posting the funds for his immediate release."

Someone in the audience gasped at the exorbitant amount flashing on the TranScreen above the justice counselors.

Justice Counselor Gabari nodded at Defense Counselor Harlowe. "Very well. You may stand and answer questions for your client. Queen Vivant, our justice chamber welcomes you. You have the first choice of seating."

Defense Counselor Harlowe smiled pityingly at Justice Counselor Gabari. "Actually, I don't think that will be necessary. We won't be before you long."

She raised one finger in the air. "However, I have a question to pose to this council." She looked up at Justin and smiled. "Was my client read his rights before he was arrested and thrown into a confinement chamber?"

"Of course!" said Chief Counselor Rand. "The king's soldiers abide by strict protocol here. They're aware no Being can be brought before us without being advised of their rights!"

"I see," said Defense Counselor Harlowe. "May I see the arrest transcript?"

"It's right here!" he said, entering data into the system. He went pale after he read the screen.

"Chief Counselor Rand? We don't have all day. What does the transcript say?"

His reddened. "Well...uh...I'm afraid it doesn't say he was advised of his rights."

Defense Counselor Harlowe smiled and said, "But isn't that Code 925 of Section 1225? Any Being under arrest shall be first advised of their rights under any planet orbiting around The One's realm. Am I correct in properly quoting the code?"

"Yes, you're correct," he said tightly.

"Are the soldiers who arrested my client here with us now?"

"Yes, they are," said Chief Counselor Rand. He nodded at two soldiers sitting in the audience. "Stand before this council!"

"I'm Captain Josin. I'm the arresting officer of Dr. Ascencio."

"I don't see where he was properly advised of his rights in this report. Would you care to enlighten us?"

The captain withered under the chief counselor's censuring tone. "I—I guess I forgot. Everything was so hectic after we found the Callidut in his office and—"

"So you didn't advise my client of Code 925?"

"No, I didn't."

"I see. Well, since my client's civilian rights were violated, I call for his immediate release and suspension of all charges brought against him."

Chief Counselor Rand's lips thinned. He nodded to Justice Counselor Gabari.

"Dr. Justin Ascencio, this council suspends the charge of drug trading and the charge of murder times two. You're free to go."

Chief Counselor Rand nodded toward another soldier. "Release him."

Justin breathed a sigh of relief when the bonds were removed from his wrists and ankles. Solemnly, he followed Queen Vivant and Defense Counselor Harlowe out of the justice chamber. Once they were outside, he said, "I need to get back to the institute. I left something important there."

"I have it right here, Dr. Ascencio," said Fawn.

Relief flowed through him. "How did you know I was being arraigned?"

"Everyone knows everything here. I wanted to be here and I figured you'd want this." Handing him the backpack, she said, "I didn't look inside."

"Thank you."

"No need for thanks. I'm just glad you're free. I know you're innocent. We all do. But until we figure out what's going on, it's best if you keep your distance from the institute."

"But—"

She held up a hand. "Whoever is after you won't stop until they finish what they've started. We don't want the patients to get antsy and decide to receive care from other planets. Please understand I'm protecting the institute's reputation while looking out for your safety."

Justin sighed. "As long as you believe I didn't do it, that's more than I can ask for."

"I believe in you, Justin. I always have. We'll find the answers. Don't worry."

"Thank you, Fawn. Please tell everyone I'll miss them."

She winked at him. "It won't be for long. You'll be back before you know it."

Bowing to Queen Vivant, she said, "In a while, Your Highness."

"I'd better get home. Hopefully, I can lay low until everything dies down," said Justin.

Queen Vivant raised her palm to the legal counselor. "Thank you, Harlowe. Here's a bonus for a job well done."

Her smile was brighter than the stars when she saw the amount. Bowing graciously, she said, "Thank you, Your Highness! I'm going to buy so many shoes, I'll need a bigger closet!"

The queen nodded toward her heels. "I love the ones you're wearing."

"By The One! I can't wait to tell everyone Queen Vivant complimented *my* shoes! And I love yours too, My Queen. Thank you for this blessing, and please contact me if you need me again."

"Thank you, Counselor Harlowe. Enjoy your shopping spree," said Justin.

"You're welcome, Prince Justin. That was fun!"

Justin laughed when she bowed and headed for a TravelCraft. When the craft was out of sight, he directed his attention to Queen Vivant. "I'm thrown for a loop. You're the last person I expected to help me."

She raised an amused brow. "I know."

"Is it rude to ask why you're here? I'm not one of your favorite Beings, you know?"

She stared at him for a long moment. "No, it isn't rude. I'll make this plain. I wasn't there for you when you were born. But I am now. Like it or not, you're an Amorous prince, and that makes you my family. My sister was devastated when you were torn apart. I wasn't going to allow it to happen again. No need to head for the cottage. You're not staying on JanIus."

"No? Where am I going?"

"To Revani."

Pivoting from his stunned expression, she strolled toward a huge craft bearing Platirius's crest. He felt someone's eyes on him and turned to find King Leighton watching from a distance. Then it hit him. Neglecting to advise him of his rights hadn't been an accident. The king had protected him. He nodded when Justin saluted him.

"Are you coming?" Queen Vivant tossed over her shoulder. "You don't want to keep Queen Revari waiting."

Domi was finishing up with her last patient when King Asa entered the medical chamber. As he crossed the foyer, a hush fell over the staff.

A sinking feeling formed in the pit of her stomach. For reasons she couldn't understand, the day she'd dreaded had come. The king had come to fire her. He approached her, ignoring the shocked stares of the NurseForms. Quickly, they bowed and greeted him.

Breaking into a cold sweat, her trembling voice belied her usual, audacious personality. "Hello, Your Highness. What brings you here? Are you unwell?"

His sparkling gray eyes were unreadable. "I feel fine. It's about time to change shifts isn't it? I was hoping to speak with you now that your shift is over."

Grasping her TeleScreen to her chest, she set it aside and braced herself. "Of course, Your Majesty. I've just finished briefing my colleagues about my patients. I'm free now."

He nodded. "Good. Let us go."

For the better part of an hour, they explored Onzi. She thought she'd faint when he gave her a special tour of his palace. Then, they tasted a few homemade delicacies from outdoor vendors before stopping at an expensive jewelry shop. The jewelry staff bowed and warmly greeted them.

He examined several of the most expensive pieces before selecting one. "Hold out your wrist," he said, before placing an exquisite, sparkling onyx and diamond bracelet around it.

Domi gawked at the bracelet, then at the king's face. "I've never owned anything this fine in my lifespan!"

His lips held the ghost of a smile.

Domi's lips trembled. "Is this severance pay, Your Highness?"

She thought she knew how to handle most MaleForms until meeting him. His confident aloofness left her mentally frostbitten. General Lyric's warning came flooding back. She'd need to be careful around him.

"Severance pay? For what?"

Blinking back tears, she asked, "This means you're relieving me of my position, doesn't it?"

His short bark of laughter didn't help to alleviate her fears.

"Why on Onzi would I terminate you, Dominia? I've heard nothing but good things about you since you began. The gift is to say congratulations on a job well done. I wouldn't read any more into it."

She sighed with relief. "Thank you, Your Majesty."

"King Asa is fine," he said, looking over her.

She wasn't an ugly WomanForm, but much too young for his tastes. He preferred mature WomenForms with long legs and silver eyes. He shook his head, trying to relieve himself of the night he'd spent with Queen Vivant. He'd reflect on it later—alone and in the comfort of his bedroom.

"So tell me about yourself. Where are you from?"

Chapter 9

Domi shifted her attention from the bracelet. "I don't know anything about my real parents. I grew up in an orphanage before I was adopted by a family, but I never felt as if I belonged. I have an older sister who never fails to tell me I wasn't wanted."

He noted the bitterness that marred her pretty face. Nodding toward the silver necklace she wore, he said, "That doesn't look too shabby. Who gave you that?"

She lifted the small silver oval secured on the chain and bit her lip.

"My ParentForms said I was wearing it when they adopted me, but they don't know where it came from."

"Do you believe that?"

"Oh yes," she said, looking up at him. "My sister might be crass, but my ParentForms were very good to me. I had a surrogate uncle too. He visited me on my birthday every year until last year. Then he disappeared. No goodbye—nothing. Two months after he missed my birthday, I received a small transmission of funds, but I never heard from him again. I think he's dead."

"It sounds as if you're used to taking care of yourself."

"Yes, My King. I never had a choice. My life has always been hard, but it's getting better."

She smiled. "I'm proud I was chosen for a scholarship and managed to finish medical school. It was the hardest thing I've ever done, but I did it. I received a good education and made solid friends. No one can take that from me."

Alarmed, her green eyes flew to his. "I hope I'm not speaking out of place, Your Majesty?"

Her knees nearly buckled when he smiled at her.

"No. My MotherForm was a spirited soul before she passed. I've never been put off by it. I'm in the mood for ice cream. Would you care to get some with me?"

"I'd be honored, My King."

King Asa smiled at her. "Good. Maybe we can figure out where you came from and how you got that necklace, hm?"

Domi couldn't speak. Beings had avoided her for as long as she could remember. No one wanted to be friends with a ChildForm without roots. Now the king of Onzi was buying her presents and sharing his company with her. She hoped it wasn't a trick. She'd been let down so many times, she didn't think she could stand another disappointment.

Sergeant Kiana ran to Queen Revari's bed chamber and knocked.

"My Queen, they've arrived! The prince is coming across the courtyard with Queen Vivant!"

Queen Revari jumped out of her chair and rushed to don her nightgown.

"May I enter, Your Highness?"

"Yes! And find my slippers!"

She spotted him when he stepped off Queen Vivant's enormous personal craft. There was her son, safe and headed straight for her. Queen Revari ran faster than she'd ever run in her lifespan. If anyone thought her nine-inch heels would slow her down, they were wrong.

She didn't stop running until she reached him. When he opened his arms and embraced her, she held him, thanking The One for allowing him to return to her.

"Hello, Mama. I'm sorry if I worried you."

"You're my baby. It's my job to worry about you."

He grunted softly. "Mom, you're crushing my ribs again."

Reluctantly, she released him and stepped back to gaze up at him. "Sorry."

"It's alright. Seeing your face is a lot better than staring at those fancy walls when I was locked up."

"You were held inside the palace. King Leighton knew better than to put you in his confinement chamber. He's already on my bad side."

Queen Vivant approached them with the princesses and the elite members of the Vivacians in tow.

"He was also smart enough to inform his guards not to read Prince Justin his rights. The justice council was forced to drop the charges and release him," said Queen Vivant.

Gallium and General Legend came running up to them. Queen Vivant bit down a spark of jealousy when General Legend embraced Justin.

"I'm so happy to see you!" Cupping his face, she stood back to examine him. "Are you okay? Are you hurt? Did they feed you well?"

"I'm fine, Aunt Legend. They served a good supper, but I was too upset to eat. I'm just glad to be free."

"I've analyzed all of the Callidut samples King Leighton sent over," said Gallium. "I was right. It didn't come from here, but we already knew that. It's a piss-poor imitation of mine. I'm not surprised it killed someone. It was mixed with synthetic ingredients, sugar, and soil."

"Let's talk about it inside," said Queen Revari. "Have one of the corporals alert the dining staff. I want soup and sandwiches sent up for us. We're going to stay up until we get to the bottom of what's going on."

She turned to Queen Vivant. "I'd like for you and the Vivacians to stay overnight too. I have plenty of room for everyone. Don't worry about clothing or toiletries. In the morning, we'll have breakfast together."

Queen Vivant hesitated, casting Gallium a wary glance.

"There's no need to bring the Callidut samples out of the research chamber. You won't be anywhere near it," Gallium assured her.

Princess Tarah squeezed her mother's hand. "That's good to know. I don't want my mother to be hurt again."

"My sister brought my son home. Do you think I'd repay her by getting her addicted again?" asked Queen Revari.

Princess Tarah lowered her eyes. "No, Aunt Revari."

"These aren't normal circumstances, but our family name and perhaps worse are at stake. If we don't band together now, we may not get another chance. Let us go."

She spun on her expensive heels with Justin, leaving the others to follow her into the palace.

After thick bowls of wild rice and mushroom soup, roast beef sandwiches, and slices of peach pie à la mode were consumed, Gallium wrote on the enlarged TranScreen, BEEMAN.

"This is what he calls himself," said Gallium. "You say you first noticed him when he stopped you from stepping in the hole? About when was this, Prince Justin?"

"Justin," he muttered, stirring his spoon in the last of his soup.

"I'll never get used to the 'prince' angle. Yes, it was around three months ago. Then weird things started happening, and everything went downhill."

General Lyric listened carefully as he rattled off the list of terrible things that had transpired in the institute.

"And he reacted so strangely when he saw my necklace. That was the night I found the nightwear under your bed."

"What nightwear?" asked Justin and Queen Revari simultaneously.

"Mother," said Justin softly.

"You mean you and her are still—"

"Mama, if you're going to start, I'll take my chances on JanIus."

Queen Revari glared at General Lyric, but kept silent.

"I found a pair of nightwear that wasn't mine under your bed," General Lyric told him.

"If he's been inside your cottage, then it was right that you came here," said Gallium. "It means he can go to and from without detection. That confirms my suspicion he uses black magic to cover his tracks. You can't return to JanIus until we find him."

Justin swore. "So much has happened. I promised Tautumn I'd find out what happened to his father! He's probably been looking for me."

"Don't worry about the ChildForm," said Queen Revari. "I've sent DeathFunds to the Overmills."

Justin plunked his spoon into his bowl. "The triplets' father is dead?"

"Yes, and the Overmills are handling it. They're safe. No need to worry about them."

Justin sighed. He was relieved to hear the triplets were doing well. He looked forward to seeing them again.

Turning to General Lyric, he said, "So that's why you were so cold when I dropped you off. Lyric, you know I'd never do something like that!"

"I'm sorry. I was just so angry."

"You should've talked to me about it." He paused. "Wait a minute. What do you mean, 'still', Mama? Have you been monitoring our relationship?"

Queen Revari rolled her eyes, refusing to answer.

A light dawned on Justin. "It was you who sent Fawn to Earth to get me, wasn't it?"

The queen crossed her legs. "No one can ever accuse you of being dumb, can they, son?"

Justin looked at Gallium, who looked just as confused as he felt. "I see you kept it from Gallium. Why would you do that, Mama? Why bring me to JanIus and why use Fawn?"

Silence.

"You thought she and I would get closer, didn't you?"

"What's wrong with a mother hoping her son will find a good WomanForm?"

"Mama! She's twenty summers!"

"And? So are you in our years!"

"Why doesn't she remember bringing me to JanIus?"

With a heavy sigh, she asked, "Do we have to discuss this now?"

"Yes, we do!"

She threw up her hands. "Fine. Fawn, and the other students opted to be a part of experiments if a situation warranted it."

"What kind of experiments?"

"We've been traveling to Earth for generations, but Dr. Barrios's last mission corrupted his mind. It scarred him. We developed a device to wipe out memories once our Beings returned to the galaxy to prevent it from happening again. That way, we could eliminate any trauma."

She looked into his eyes. "Fawn has no memories of Earth and that's how I wanted it. She voluntarily signed up to join the program. She became a ParaNurture physician and my son is back in the galaxy with me. It was a win-win."

"When will you stop interfering in my life?!"

She smacked the arm of the chair. "I interceded at the right time. Do you think I'd allow the Humans to lock you away in a lab and experiment on you?"

"You had no problem experimenting on Fawn!" he shouted.

She shrugged. "She gave her permission. No one forced her to."

Gallium cleared his throat. "Excuse me, My Queen, but I think it's more important to find out who this Beeman is. He's out there executing the second part of his plan now that Prince Justin isn't locked up."

171

She waved her hand. "Go on." Casting a pointed look at Justin, she said, "I'll be quiet." Training her attention on the TranScreen, she stared at the letters. Her fingers snapped together.

"Gallium? Do you remember when we went to that nightclub a couple of years ago?"

Justin's eyebrow raised. "You go to clubs?"

"Shh," said General Legend, giving him a soft pinch.

Queen Revari leaned forward. "King Belial carved that into the beverage bar."

Gallium looked at the letters and narrowed his eyes.

"Beeman," he said. "Beeman..." He swore. "By The One. How did this slip past me?"

"What does it mean?" asked General Legend.

Gallium wrote *Bee over Man. Bee/Man.* "Beelzebub over Man. King Belial worships Satan. His mother was a sorceress who taught him everything he knows." He wanted to punch something. "He's been in plain sight all of this time. King Belial is Beeman!"

"Who's King Belial?" asked Justin.

"An insane MaleForm who inherited Platz after his father died. I accosted his father, King Noham, the night the students graduated. We—" She cast a side eye at Justin "—experimented on him so he'd report to us if Belial was really dead, but it didn't work. He tried to escape and drowned. When a light rose out of him and shot over Platz, I knew then Belial had faked his death."

Justin leaned forward. "Why would he fake dying?"

"He broke into my palace and stole from me," said Queen Revari. "A few pieces of jewelry your father bought for me in Cuba, an old photo of Oliver and I when I was pregnant, and some of my...nightwear. He fancies himself in love with me. At least what his warped mind considers love."

"He sounds crazy and obsessed," said Justin.

"I've never paid him the slightest attention. He's proposed to me several times, but I always said no."

"He's also jealous," said Gallium. "He found out Prince Justin is your son and devised a plan to take him out. Maybe he blames him for you rejecting him."

"He's so insane it actually makes sense," said Queen Revari.

"Alright. Now we have a clear picture of who Beeman is. Have you had any more dreams about King Carlomon?"

Justin perked up. "Yes! He spoke to me the last time I saw him." He described the stone.

"It's the CarogueStone," said General Legend. "He never took it off."

"Well, apparently he only wore half of it. He said before he became king, he gave the other half of it to his first love. He didn't say her name, but the letters LA appeared to me."

"LA?" echoed General Legend. She gasped. "Lady Alarah?! King Carlomon and Lady Alarah were together?!"

Lady Alarah, thought Queen Vivant. *Where have I heard that name before?* Her breath caught. *The WomanForm who laughed when my mother died! That beast is Lyric's mother? By*

The One. And she's still locked away in the Flames of Justice. As she deserves.

"It has to be her. She's the only Coldarian with the initials," said Gallium. "I saw her visit the palace a lot. One night, there was a commotion, and the soldiers escorted her out. They must have dated before each of them married."

"Why would my mother be asked to leave the palace?" asked General Lyric.

Gallium met General Legend's eyes.

General Lyric looked from one to the other. "What do you know about my mother?"

"General Lyric," said General Legend. "I know we've had our differences, but I'd never say anything hurtful about your mother. She was...a difficult Being to get along with."

General Lyric's eyes narrowed. "Meaning?"

"She was haughty and vicious," said Gallium. "She thought she was better than everyone else. And she made it her mission to make trouble for others."

"What kind of trouble?" asked General Lyric.

"It's in the past, General Lyric."

"Well, the past has come back to bite us, hasn't it? I want to know how my mother is involved in all of this."

Gallium nodded at her. "Your necklace. The one King Belial had a reaction to. She gave it to you, didn't she?"

Unconsciously, the general touched her necklace. "Yes."

"I think the stone is inside of it."

"Only part of the stone," said Justin. "Great-grandfather said she split the stone between her daughters."

"Daughters? I'm the only daughter she has."

Justin looked at her sadly. "No, Lyric. She had another daughter. You have a sister out there somewhere."

"Justin, don't you think I'd know if I had a sister? It's true my mother was pregnant when I was young, but she said she lost it."

"That's what she said," said Gallium. "But her actions tell a different story. If the king told Justin that another daughter has the other half of the CarogueStone, then it's true. And we have to find it. It was never meant to be separated."

His eyes held General Lyric's. "It didn't hold any power when he gifted it to her, but after he became king, it became Coldarius's lifeforce. Had it been whole, King Carlomon's life might've been spared. He would've been strong enough to fight off King Dubian."

Justin wrapped his arm around General Lyric. "It's okay. Once we find her, maybe she can tell us what happened to her."

General Lyric nodded. She felt numb inside.

What other secrets don't I know about you, Mother?

"May we see the stone, Lyric?" asked Queen Vivant.

General Lyric removed the necklace and opened the clasp to reveal a brilliant, tiny topaz. It glowed and sparkled under the lighting.

"It's beautiful," said Princess Tyre.

"Great-grandfather said when Coldarius exploded, pieces flew through Space and landed in different places. King Dubian stole his necklace after he murdered him. One piece lies in the center of JanIus's core, and another is lodged in the center of Earth, just before the door of Hell."

Queen Revari looked stricken.

"What is it?" asked Queen Vivant.

"I sold grandfather's CarogueStone to King Belial just before King Dubian died. I didn't know it belonged to him!"

"So that's how King Belial got his hands on it," said Gallium. "And it gives him tremendous power. That's how he knew Prince Justin and you were linked, My Queen."

Queen Vivant sat forward. "So that's where all of Father's belongings went? You sold them?"

"So?" Queen Revari shot back. "It's not as if you wanted any keepsakes to remind you of him! But I...I didn't realize the CarogueStone would give him access to Justin." She buried her face in her hands. "It's my fault he went after him!"

Justin squeezed her shoulder. "No, it isn't. There's only one who's responsible for his actions—him. I don't blame you for selling your father's things."

"Neither do I," Queen Vivant admitted. "He stole your photo. With or without the CarogueStone, he would've become fixated on Justin. Don't blame yourself, Revari."

"JanIus is a piece of Coldarius," said Gallium. "After it exploded, a part of it hit a small, uninhabited planet and created life on it. I can plow through it and retrieve the shard with no problem. But..."

General Legend sensed his hesitation. "But what?" she asked. "What's wrong?"

"Earth drains my powers. I can get to the center of it and get the other piece but..."

Exasperated, General Legend said, "And? Out with it already!"

"I might not have enough strength to return to Space."

"Then I guess you won't be going to get it then!"

"Legend, I'm the only one who can! If we don't find all the pieces of the CarogueStone and rejoin it, King Belial will take the whole galaxy! Look here," he said, turning his attention to the TranScreen. "He owns Platz. Here's JanIus, Onzi, Revani, and Platirius. I'm betting he'll try to take JanIus first and absorb it to get the other piece of the stone."

Justin watched the mock planets absorb into Platz on the screen.

"If he succeeds, he'd be strong enough to come for Platirius, then Earth. After that, he'd have most of the stone. His next stop would be swooping in on Onzi, then Revani. The other planets would just get caught up in the shuffle! I have to go, Legend!"

"I'm hearing none of this! I won't let you risk your life! Maybe there's another way we can retrieve the rest of the pieces. Then we won't need the one on Earth!"

"Great-grandfather said we need all the pieces to set him free. It's all or nothing," said Justin.

"Then that settles it," said Gallium.

"Gallium!" cried General Legend.

"Gallium, what? Our king needs us. We failed him when we didn't stop King Dubian from taking Coldarius. My mother died in that freeze! So did yours! I'm not going to stand by and watch another crazy MaleForm destroy what's left of our race! I'd rather die than see King Belial control any part of Coldarius!"

Angry tears smarted in her eyes, but he said, "I'm going, Legend. We have a duty to our king. End of discussion!"

Queen Revari placed on hand on General Legend's shoulder. "I don't remember anything about Coldarius, but Gallium is right. We have to do what my grandfather asks to protect the galaxy. There's no other way."

General Legend bowed her head and stormed off. Queen Vivant turned her head, hiding a smile.

Gallium sighed.

"She'll be alright," said Queen Revari. "Let's all get some rest. In the morning, we'll discuss how to take down King Belial over breakfast."

J ustin's first breakfast with his extended galactic family was a solemn affair. General Legend sullenly added food to her plate, refusing to speak to Gallium.

General Lyric was despondent over the news about her mother, and he was still upset she hadn't discussed finding the nightwear under his bed with him. He hated when she shut down instead of expressing her feelings. To him, having open communication was the healthiest way for their relationship to survive.

Platters of scrambled eggs, ham, bacon, and beef sausages were passed around the table. Queen Vivant's buttermilk pancakes and lighter-than-air waffles were a hit with everyone. They were served with thick maple syrup, strawberry, and blueberry sauces. The dining staff added apple and cherry fritters to the already groaning table.

An array of diverse palates called for avocado toast, arepas, chorizo, pan con chicharrónes—sandwiches made with fried pork belly, sweet potato, and salsa criolla—a spicy onion relish. Justin was pleased to see café con leche—coffee with milk—and pan tostado—toasted bread—along with gallo pinto—rice and black beans with buttery cheese and plantains.

Captain Kourtney pushed back her plate and sighed. "My uniform will be so tight, I'll have to peel it off."

Sergeant Alicia said, "Mine too, but I have a feeling we'll need the energy."

"How will we find the WomanForm who has the other necklace?" asked Princess Teenah. "We don't know what she looks like or where she is. It'll be like trying to find a needle in a haystack!"

Queen Vivant tapped a finger on the table. "What about the students who enrolled in our ParaNurture program? There were over fourteen hundred. If she were a student, that'll narrow it down."

Queen Revari took another shot of Cuban espresso. "That's a good idea, but it'll take time to get through all the names."

"Maybe not," said Justin. "I know someone who's very observant."

Pulling out his TeleScreen, he placed a call to the institute. "Hello, you've reached the Azini Institute. This is Dr. Azini speaking."

"Hi, Fawn!"

"Hello, Justin! How are you feeling?"

"Much better than yesterday. Hey, I have a question. You spent a lot of time around most of the students in your program. Do you remember anyone who—" He turned to General Lyric.

"—May I see your necklace, love? Did you see anyone who wore a necklace like this?"

He held the necklace up for her to see.

Fawn stared at it. "Does it open?"

"Yeah!"

"And it has a small blue stone?"

Everyone sat still, focusing on Fawn.

"Yes, how did you know?"

Fawn started to say something when a loud explosion sounded. JanIus's emergency siren blared loudly.

Fawn jumped up. "We're under attack!" she shouted.

Everyone stood when they heard, "ATTENTION, ALL THE KING'S SOLDIERS MUST PREPARE FOR BATTLE IMMEDIATELY! THE PLATZARIANS ARE ATTACKING US!"

King Belial stood high above JanIus, looking down at the terrified Beings running for cover. He leaned his head back, drawing air deep into his lungs. "Father! The time has come to avenge you and take what's mine!"

He pointed his BrainStaff at the palace. "Starting now."

"I have to go, Justin!" said Fawn before disconnecting the transmission.

"It's King Belial! He's come for JanIus just like you said, Gallium! We need to get over there!"

"There's no way in hell I'm letting you go!" exclaimed Queen Revari. "You're not a JanIan! Let King Leighton handle his own affairs!"

"Mom, I've been living there for almost two years. I know those Beings. I have friends there! I can't just leave them hanging."

"It's their king's responsibility to protect JanIus, not yours!"

Justin took her by the hands and lifted her to her feet. "Do you want me to be a pampered prince forever, or do you want me to stand on my own? We can't let King Belial get his hands on that stone! It will make him too powerful!"

Queen Revari opened her mouth to protest when a bulletin flashed across the large TranScreen.

Breaking! Platirius is on fire!

The Amorous sisters' eyes flew to the screen to see an enormous statue of Queen Dellah falling to the ground.

"Mother!" shouted Queen Vivant. "Come! We have to get to Platirius!"

"Revaltians!" bellowed Queen Revari, "Prepare for Platirius!"

She looked up at Justin.

"I'll be okay, Mom. Just go. Protect Platirius."

He kissed her and General Lyric before running to get suited up.

"Legend," said Gallium. "Legend, please look at me."

She refused.

"General Legend!"

"This isn't Coldarius," she snapped. "I'm not under your command anymore," she said.

He placed both hands on her shoulders. "Coldarius will always live in us. It was your planet and mine. It's where we fought together and made love for the first time. Our mothers died in the snow."

She couldn't stop the tears from spilling.

Tilting her head to look at him, he said, "Being by your side in love and war has been the honor of my life." He held her in his arms when she lost control. "Legend, do you remember the rainbow roses I gave you?"

Not trusting herself to speak, she nodded.

"Well," he said, resting his chin on the top of her head. "If I don't make it back, I'll send the stones in a rainbow rose. You won't have to look for it. Your soul will connect with mine right before you see it."

She grabbed him around the waist, squeezing him as hard as she could. Stepping back to look up into his face, she said, "I love you, General Barrios." She sniffed. "And I'll never forgive you if you don't come back to me!"

He grinned at her lovely face. "Never is a long time, General."

They kissed a long, sweet kiss that was filled with longing and the promise of tomorrow.

She felt a swift, gentle pat on her bottom. "Get out there. I'll be back to kiss all of your bruises."

Reluctantly, she let go of him and ran to join her team.

By the time Justin finished changing into his armor, the WomenForms had left. "You ready, Gallium?"

"I stay ready, Prince Justin."

Justin eyed his impressive blue and platinum armor. "Then let us go, General Barrios!"

JanIus was in flames when they reached it. The green crafts of the Platzarians hovered over burning buildings and bodies strewn on the ground.

"Why run?" shouted King Belial. "Stand and give your new king the proper respect!"

Laughing, he grabbed Tio with one hand. "Bow to your new king, ChildForm. There's nothing I despise more than insolent little brats not knowing their place!"

"Get Belial," said Gallium. "I'm going after the stones!"

Justin watched him jump from the craft and plow headfirst into the ground below. Energized by the ancient power of Coldarius, he tunneled deeper into the soil until he spotted the stone.

"There you are!" said Gallium as he grabbed it. "Can't stop now." He shot out of JanIus, spinning toward Earth at lightning speed.

"Put him down, Beeman!" shouted Justin.

King Belial turned and looked at him. "Well, look at you all dressed up for your DeathCeremony! Did your MotherForm buy that nice BrainStaff for you?"

"My mother isn't your concern," snarled Justin.

A strange light entered King Belial's eye. "She's always my concern. She's my sun, moon, and stars."

Flinging Tio to the ground, he advanced toward Justin.

"Run, Tio!" shouted Justin.

"I'll slice him up later," said King Belial. "Right now, I have something more pressing on my mind. Cutting out your eyes and sending them to Queen Revari." He cocked his head. "Then again, I might just add them to my pot and see what spells I can conjure. No use in taking your brain—you're half Human." He nodded toward the water. "Those pelicans are smarter than you."

With his sword and BrainStaff raised, Justin moved closer to him. "You thought you were smarter than everyone, but killing Ms. Dill and framing me was a mistake!"

King Belial assessed him emotionlessly. "Yeah. That was fun. No one misses a little whore like her. No one cared when she died." He flexed his shoulders. "Some Beings don't deserve to live."

"Finally, we agree on something," said Justin.

"King Belial!" It was King Leighton. "If you've come to take my head, you're in for a surprise!"

King Belial looked from him to Justin, pointing his sword at the king. "You think I can't beat you and him?" He doubled over in laughter. "Now that's the funniest thing I've heard this morning. You're no fighter, Leighton. You never were."

King Leighton raised his BrainStaff, waving him over. "Come and test me then, you one-eyed ox."

The smile disappeared from King Belial's face. "Now, why stoop to hurt my feelings? It's too early to act like a cunt, Leighton."

"No one would know it better than you, Belial. Are you finished?"

King Belial balanced his BrainStaff on his thigh. "Nope."

He attacked King Leighton with a swiftness that caught Justin off guard. Carefully measuring his timing, he leapt into the fight. King Leighton and Justin hammered at King Belial, who returned their blows with a viciousness Justin had never encountered.

The Platzarians and JanIans fought in the blazing sun rising high over the hills overlooking JanIus. King Belial and King Leighton tumbled toward the ground, landing hard on the purple grass.

Out of the corner of his eye, Justin saw Fawn displaying the flawless skills she'd demonstrated on Earth. One by one, she took off heads without pausing. He focused his attention back on King Belial just in time to see a large boulder flying toward him.

It hit him in the chest, knocking him out of the sky. He commanded his BrainStaff to materialize a platform to break his fall. Without breaking stride, he flew to King Belial, landing a series of hard jabs to his skull and face. King Leighton sliced at his legs and stabbed his sword into his foot.

King Belial grimaced. "Rude of you to mess up my white shoes!" he said, slicing open King Leighton's face. He dragged him by the hair and shaved off his long locks with his sword.

"There! Now you finally look like a MaleForm!" he said, giving him a vicious kick to the groin while landing a sharp elbow to Justin's mouth. Tasting his own blood, Justin shook his head to clear it.

King Belial brought his BrainStaff down hard on Justin's skull. "You're * half * Human * so * you * can't * take * these * blows * like * me!"

An expert kick to Justin's chin sent him flying into a building. He fell face-first in the dirt.

"Justin!" cried Fawn, running over to him.

Slowly, King Belial walked to where King Leighton lay and raised his sword. "You've put up a good fight, but it's time to end this now."

He raised his sword in the air.

"Noooooooooooooo!" screamed Justin.

Chapter 10

The WomenForms stared in shock around the courtyard.

"What on Platirius is going on?" asked Queen Vivant. "We saw Mother's statue falling to the ground! It's untouched."

Queen Revari looked around and frowned. Something was amiss.

"My Queen," said Major Sonee, coming out of the palace with her twin sister, Sergeant Thea. What's wrong?"

"We saw Platirius being attacked on the TranScreen!"

The twins looked at each other. "Everything has been peaceful since you left for Revani."

King Asa appeared out of the shadows. "There's evil magic at work here. I saw the bulletin too."

Queen Vivant looked past him to the troops he'd brought with him.

"There's more," he said, pointing to the sky. "I figured we'd need them."

Queen Vivant approached him. "I don't mean to sound ungrateful, but you didn't need to come, Asa. This is my fight."

"Yes, I did. Where else would I be?"

Noting the not-so-subtle intimacy shimmering between her sister and King Asa, Queen Revari raised an eyebrow, but kept silent.

"What do we do now, My Queen?" asked Captain Kourtney.

Queen Vivant looked up at the sky. "We'll stay. I have a feeling someone planted a ruse to get us here. I won't leave Platirius unattended until I find out what it is. Let us go inside the palace."

King Asa nodded at Colonel Brazo. "Stay on alert. If anything happens, call me immediately."

Colonel Brazo saluted him. "Yes, My King!"

King Belial held his sword to King Leighton's neck. "Call me your king and I'll make your death quick and painless."

King Leighton spat blood. "Never. And you'll never take this planet."

King Belial laughed. "No? What am I holding to your juggler? A baguette? And you're wounded so badly, you can't get up. Wait, my mistake. Let's fix that."

He plunged his sword deep into King Leighton's belly.

Amused by King Leighton's screams, he said, "Alright! There's the spirit! See? I knew we'd get there, friend!"

King Belial smiled evilly at him. "Thanks for inviting me to breakfast, but I have a lunch date with Queen Vivant."

He raised his sword high in the air. Fawn and Justin hit the back of his head with a combined hard blow, sending him sprawling to the ground, breathing harshly.

Justin stretched his hand to King Leighton. "My King, let's get you to safety."

"No," said King Leighton. He removed his hand from the fatal wound in his torso. "There's no time. You can't let him take JanIus. You have to kill me before I bleed out."

"What? No! I can't do that!"

"Please, Prince Justin! You have to! Don't let my father's planet be taken."

Blood spattered on his armor when he coughed. "We're the last...descendants of Coldarius... You have to preserve King Carlomon's legacy. Please do it before he gets his strength back. Take my head."

Justin shook his head. "All this time, you knew who I was?"

"Yes. Queen Revari trusted me to protect you. I tried my best, but I failed. Don't let me fail my subjects! It's your time now. Take my place as their king."

"He's moving, Justin," warned Fawn. "You have to do it now!"

King Leighton nodded at him and smiled. "May The One protect you."

Justin looked up at the lavender sky before severing King Leighton's head. He braced himself against JanIus's essence flowing from its former king to him. An illuminating glow rose over them. King Leighton's BrainStaff shattered and formed anew. Justin grabbed it from the air, raised it high above his head, and absorbed all of JanIus's memories. The JanIan soldiers formed a circle around him, bowing to their new king.

"All hail the new king of JanIus—King Justin!" bellowed Captain Josin.

Thick, smoky clouds blanketed the sun while thunder and lightning ripped through the sky. King Carlomon's voice rang out among Space.

"Enter the king. Enter...the...king..."

"I'll right all the wrongs, Great-Grandfather. I promise."

"No, you won't," declared King Belial, getting to his feet.

He hit King Justin and Fawn with a blast that knocked them out cold.

King Justin awakened to a pounding in his skull and the sound of a shovel hitting dirt. Alarmed, he tried to move his arms and legs, but couldn't feel them. He watched in horror when King Belial tossed the shovel aside and dragged an old, bloody, badly damaged DeathCraft from around a mountain.

He lowered King Justin's body into it and said, "This place has been abandoned for years. It's an old graveyard where Platirians used to bury their dead."

He knocked on the DeathCraft. "It's made of good material that has lasted all this time. I'll bet King Dubian didn't expect Prince Dimaro to escape it. I've drugged you up good enough, so you won't be breaking out of anything. Since you're half-Human, you won't last nearly as long as he did. You'll be dead in a few hours."

King Justin grimaced. "He buried his own brother alive. Now you're here, emulating him. You don't see how demented this is?"

King Belial's fully dilated pupil made him look crazed. "Well, it's like I told you, King Justin. Sometimes, we dig holes so deep that we can't get out of them. I call that irony."

"You were behind all of those horrible things that happened at the institute. Why are you doing this to me? What have I done to you?"

"You were born," said King Belial. "You've been my enemy since the first moment you took a breath in your lungs."

"That doesn't make any sense. Do you hear how you sound?"

King Belial's demented eye bore into his. "What? Crazy? You mean like your grandfather, who walked these grounds, whispering to himself? If it weren't for you, he wouldn't have locked up his daughter. You're responsible for everything that went wrong in her life. Her future was doomed the second she stole that craft and crashed it on Earth."

He wiped the sweat from his brow. "You think I'm wicked, but I'm not. I'm an angel assigned by Satan to avenge past wrongs. It all begins and ends with you. Your death will usher in a new reckoning. Mine."

He dragged King Justin toward the hole. "Well, enough chitter chatter. Let's get you in now so you can die."

King Justin tried to struggle, but couldn't move. King Belial tossed him into the hole as if he weighed no more than a sack of potatoes. Quickly, he began shoveling dirt on top of him. King Justin furiously shook his head, trying to dislodge the dirt that was mounting on top of him.

King Belial paused and looked over at Fawn. "Don't worry about her. By the time she comes to, you'll be dead, and I'll be king of the universe once I get my hands on the rest of those stones."

When the hole was filled, he threw the shovel down. Forming a mock salute, he said, "Farewell, King of JanIus!"

Gallium knew the journey to Earth's core would be difficult, but he never imagined the suffering he'd endure. Demons had mercilessly attacked him from all sides. The deeper he traveled through the center of Earth, the more his power weakened. His hair turned white, and his skin withered and wrinkled before his eyes.

Keep going! You have to make it. You can't let your king down again.

The closer he got to Hell, the harder it became to breathe. Blood gushed from wounds to his head, spilling into his eyes.

Finally! There it is!

Reaching for the stone with one hand, he pierced a demon with his sword. Enraged, its shrill scream echoed through the tunnel.

Got it!

The demons flew away when his hand closed over the stone. He held it to his pounding heart before opening it to peer at the small gem. After adding it to the one he'd retrieved from JanIus, he sighed. It was finally over. Closing his eyes to savor all of the memories he'd made with the Beings he loved, a tear trickled from his eye.

I'll never see my lovely Legend again.

Far away in the distance, he thought he heard Queen Dellah's voice.

"Well done. You can let go now, Gallium. Come home..."

Closing his fists over the jewels, he willed his mind to transmit them through time and Space to his wife. Feeling his heartbeat slow, then stop, he crossed his arms over his chest and smiled.

What a wild ride! I love you, General Legend Guilde-Barrios.

Thunder and lightning ripped through the night sky. The sweet fragrance of Queen Vivant's rose garden permeated the air. No one made a sound as they waited for King Belial's next move. General Legend was standing by a massive window when she felt a burst of warm energy embrace her. A rainbow rose grew to maturity on a vine.

"Nooooooo," she wailed.

Queen Revari jumped up from the divan and ran to her. "What? What is it?" Her eyes spotted the rose slowly opening. "Oh no," she said. "Gallium."

"Gallium," sobbed General Legend.

General Lyric ran to the window and saw the small jewels inside the rose. Carefully, she retrieved them and added them to her necklace.

"That makes three," she told Queen Vivant. "All we need now is the one that King Belial has and the one from the other WomanForm." She turned and squeezed General Legend's hand. "I'm so sorry, Legend."

Unconsolable, General Legend cried on her shoulder. "Lyric! He can't be gone! He can't be!"

Queen Vivant didn't feel an ounce of sympathy for her half-sister, but her heart shattered for Gallium. They hadn't had enough time to mend their differences. On a night as silent as a tomb, all heads bowed in mourning for Gallium.

F awn opened her eyes to the sound of scratching.

"King Justin!" she called. "King Justin, where are you?"

She stood still and listened. The sound was coming from underneath the ground.

"By The One! That crazy bastard!"

She rushed to the mound of dirt, clawing at it. "Hold on, Your Highness! Please!"

After several minutes of furiously digging through the soil, she began to panic.

The hole is so deep! I have to get him out before he runs out of air!

Suddenly, she was lifted in the air and flung to another part of the graveyard. Jumping quickly to her feet, she unsheathed her sword and ran back toward the grave.

She stopped when she saw a MaleForm in black robes stretch his hand toward the grave and summon the DeathCraft out of the ground. It landed on the dry, dead grass with a soft *thump*. When he turned his hand, the lid flew open.

King Justin climbed out, surrounded by a platinum glow. He could feel the strength returning to his body. The stranger ran his fingers along the old, bloodstained cover before standing to look at Fawn. She almost backed away from the rage burning in his black eyes.

"I've allowed this madness to go on long enough," said King Anemi haughtily.

He disappeared, leaving Fawn stunned by what she'd witnessed. She ran to King Justin and helped him to his feet.

"Are you alright, My King?"

He looked around the graveyard. "Are you talking to me?"

Fawn's teasing smile made him feel alive again. "Yes. You're the King of JanIus, you know?"

Everything came flooding back to him. "King Belial! He's headed for Platirius!"

"He's not the only one," said Fawn.

"What do you mean?"

"Come on. I'll tell you on the way."

"I think I know where the other stone may be," said King Asa. He looked at Domi. Nodding at her, he said, "Open your necklace."

Everyone gasped when she opened it, revealing the petite, sparkling little topaz.

"Domi, your mother was Lady Alarah of Coldarius. She divided her half of the CarogueStone between you and your sister." He pointed at General Lyric. "And there she is."

Domi and General Lyric stared at each other.

"Give her the stone, Domi," ordered King Asa.

In a daze, she walked toward the general and handed it to her.

"There's so much I want to say," said Domi. "So many questions I have."

Before she could say more, a blast shot through her back.

King Belial!

He stood over her crumpled form. "I should've killed you when you were born. Better late than never."

"Domi!" cried General Lyric, unsheathing her sword. "Here you die!" she promised.

He cocked his head. "Like your mother? No, thank you. Family reunions have always bored me to tears."

He sneered at General Legend. "And I'm funny about who makes the potato salad."

"You crazy bastard!" spat Queen Revari. "You dare show your face here!"

"Why not? We'll be rolling around on these floors with me inside of you for the rest of our lifespans. Why prolong it?" he asked, swinging his sword at General Legend's head.

"Give the stones to me. King Justin won't be using them anytime soon." He smiled at Queen Revari. "I buried him in Prince Dimaro's old grave."

Enraged, she pounced on him, slicing off the tip of his nose. Together, they flew through the glass of a window.

"I can hear them fighting! We have to get to Platirius!"

"Don't worry, My King! We will!"

They ran faster down the mountain into a sea of King Belial's demonic, supernatural warriors. Fawn added her lot to the numerous swords and BrainStaffs clashing with satanic forces. King Justin flew through the air, landing on King Belial's back.

He shouted when King Belial threw him off and stabbed him in the side. Snatching the necklace from King Belial's neck, he broke it open to retrieve the CarogueStone. General Lyric rushed to give him the remaining pieces. The five small stones began glowing, then merged together in his hand.

Closing his eyes, he whispered, "Enter the king. If The One wills, enter the king!"

When the pieces were fashioned into a horn, he blew into it. Enchanting sounds rang throughout the sky, and a door in Space opened. He watched as the shadow of a MaleForm came into view.

"Enter the king..." said a voice high inside the Heavens. King Carlomon appeared, flying toward King Justin with his hand outstretched. Relieved, he jumped to his feet and took it. Once King Carlomon's spirit became flesh, his BrainStaff rose to life through a split in the courtyard. It found its master, who took the horn from King Justin and blew into it.

The lost Coldarians, scattered throughout the galaxy, paused to hear the call of their former king. Their heartbeats kept in rhythm with the seductive tunes of the CarogueStone. Soon, thousands of Coldarian soldiers flew toward Platirius, chanting a forgotten war cry.

The horn's music reached Gallium's ears. Blood began flowing into his veins again, transitioning his hair from white to black. The wrinkles melted from his skin as his eyes shot open.

"Basheelabeyyyyyyyyyyyyyy!" he called.

General Legend turned and looked toward the sky.

Gallium!

Queen Revari watched the Coldarians descend upon Platirius. Guided by an unfamiliar force, she squeezed Queen Vivant's hand and received a firm squeeze back. Hearing Gallium's call, General Legend was astonished to witness familiar colorful hues shining in Captain TamRi's eyes, but Queen Vivant proudly watched her captain shoot through Space like a star, headed for Earth.

"Alabasheeeee!" called Captain TamRi.

"Legend," shouted Queen Revari, pointing to the sky. "There! Look there!"

Gallium and Captain TamRi sped through the clouds toward Platirius—two soldiers in The One's army, prepared to battle the agents of darkness for the glory of His kingdom.

"Platirius will not fall," said King Carlomon, raising his BrainStaff. "Tonight, Coldarius has risen!"

King Belial gripped his BrainStaff so tightly, ribbons of blood ran from the wounds on his fingers. "You should've stayed dead. Your resurrection changes nothing. I'm sending Coldarius straight to Hell!"

"The only one who'll see your master is you," said King Carlomon. "You cursed yourself by possessing a power that wasn't yours. You have perverted the laws of The One. You must face judgement!"

King Justin stood beside him. "Your reign ends here."

Raising his BrainStaff and sword, King Carlomon sounded the call to attack. Warriors of spirit and flesh and blood lunged toward the wicked army, slaying everything in their paths.

The agents of darkness cut their teeth on the swords of the noble while King Anemi watched from the shadows. King Belial swung his sword at King Justin, who blocked the blow and sliced the blade of his sword through his neck.

The wicked king placed a hand on the fatal wound, surveying the blood on his hands in disbelief. "Impossible! Satan, you promised me everything!" he said, before falling to his death.

A sheen of rain and mist descended over Platirius as Platz's power was absorbed into King Justin and JanIus. A new BrainStaff materialized before him, signaling Platz's soldiers to bow to their new king. One by one, King Belial's supernatural army turned to dust and faded away, drowned in the cheers of the brave rulers and soldiers united against them.

"Lo, General Barrios!" cried Sergeant Lionus. "We've come home!"

Gallium chanted the Coldarian war cry, raising his fist in the air. All the Coldarians, past and present, sounded the call of sweet victory!

A timekeeper with numerals that no one could interpret appeared in the sky. Queen Vivant ran into King Carlomon's outstretched arms. Planting a soft kiss on her forehead, he reared back, revealing the pride shining in his eyes.

"Come, Revari!" she called. "Meet our grandfather!"

But Queen Revari remained where she was, quietly observing him. Once King Carlomon was close enough to touch, she felt a powerful wave of light and love directed toward her.

"Revari. I have missed you!" Taking her hand, he transmitted memories of the time they'd spent together at his palace. Queen Vivant held her trembling form close, allowing her to weep for a past she hadn't known existed.

"I was loved," she kept whispering. "I was loved!"

"Yes, my little one," said King Carlomon. "We loved you then and we love you still, Revari. Nothing will ever change that."

"Gallium!" cried General Legend. She ran into his arms and held on to him tightly. He lifted her in his arms, never wanting to let her go.

King Carlomon placed a soft kiss on Queen Revari's cheek. "It's time to go now," he said, handing his BrainStaff to King

Justin. "You are three times a king. Never in the galaxy's history has it been done. I am so proud of you."

King Justin felt another wave of energy flow through him when Coldarius's essence entered JanIus. Following the mysterious timekeeper's disappearance, the descendants watched their ancestor ascend to The One's realm.

Queen Vivant nodded to King Asa. He winked at her while his soldiers retrieved Domi.

"We'll take good care of her," he told Fawn. "She's one of mine now." Turning to Queen Vivant, he bowed and said, "In a while, My Queen."

Several days later

Once Platirius's grounds were immaculate again, Captain Kourtney was appointed to Colonel, while Captain TamRi received the honor of becoming Queen Vivant's Advisor.

Fawn found King Justin standing in the queen's vegetable garden. "Everything is ready on JanIus. The craft is waiting, Your Highness. Are you ready to return home now?"

He looked around at everyone. "Yes! I think a celebration is in order, don't you?"

"I could certainly use a drink. Or two," said Princess Teenah.

He smiled at her. "Then let us go!"

Surveying the new group of Coldarians who'd joined them, he said, "It would be an honor to show you to your new home."

Everyone piled into the crafts, but Queen Revari turned to Queen Vivant. "Aren't you coming?"

She shook her head. "No. I know it couldn't have ended any other way, but Platirius losing Coldarius's essence was something I didn't see coming."

"Platirius should never have owned it, Vivant."

Queen Vivant's shoulders slumped. "I know. I just feel as if Mother has left us all over again."

"No, she didn't. Our father's evil deed has been undone, and Coldarius is finally free. Did you see how happy our grandfather was? We don't have to worry about them anymore." She sighed. "I won't force you to come, but I hope you'll change your mind."

Queen Vivant wrinkled her nose at her. "Why are you being so nice to me?"

She missed Queen Revari's secretive smile when she turned and headed for her WarCraft.

Epilogue

Queen Vivant stood in the courtyard alone, overlooking the beautiful gardens. Usually, the beauty and fragrance of the blooming flowers calmed her spirits, but she couldn't shake the melancholy that had claimed her since losing Coldarius to JanIus.

"It must be hard knowing almost everyone you love has betrayed you."

She turned to face the approaching figure. "Grandfather Anemi? Where did you come from?"

King Anemi smiled. "They've taken everything you held dear. Coldarius was ripped from Platirius and has joined with JanIus. Your mother's planet. Even your faithful general has gone to be with her lover. Your daughters are celebrating the night away with King Justin, too. JanIus is basking in what should've been Platirius's glory."

"I don't see how any of this concerns you," she said coldly.

He slowly approached her.

"That's far enough," she said, taking a step backward.

He surveyed the massive grounds. "I haven't come to harm you. As long as Coldarius was a part of these grounds, your mother's lifeforce flowed within you. Now there's nothing left except bitter spirits and hard feelings."

She raised an eyebrow. "Bitter spirits? You mean you?"

He ignored the jab. "I can help you take back what's yours. The Halfling is on a high now after taking three planets. He thinks he alone is the savior of the galaxy. A half-Human taking control of one of the greatest empires that ever existed is sheer perversion. Let me help you."

Defiantly, she lifted her chin. "I'm still the Queen of Platirius and I always will be. What makes you think I need your assistance?"

He circled her. "Ah, but even queens are surrounded by mystery. Don't you want to know what really happened to General Kron?"

She eyed him suspiciously. "What would you know about that? You were rotting away when my husband died."

His captivating smile was oddly familiar. "I know exactly what happened to him. Gallium lied to you. He knows what happened too."

He looked up at the massive statue of Queen Dellah. "Gallium has always been in your sister's corner, and he always will be. He's sworn allegiance to her, and now, her half-abomination."

The sinking feeling in the pit of her stomach rose again. Fighting a wave of anxiety, she turned from him.

"In your heart you know I'm telling the truth. Queen Revari murdered your husband just as she murdered your father. She took vengeance for what happened to her Human husband."

He stood in front of her. "The murder of a royal is punishable by death. It's your mother's decree. You have a duty to uphold her laws."

She lowered her head. Tears mixed with rain on the platinum ground.

"Revari never forgave you for something that wasn't your fault. Dubian was responsible for everything, yet she unleashed her rage on you. Your daughters grew up without their father while you were forced to go on without the love of your life. Do you think that's fair?"

He reached for her. "Take my hand. Let me help you restore what was lost. Together, we'll get justice for General Kron."

"I don't know how I didn't recognize him before. Prince Dimaro had your smile."

His penetrating gaze held her captive. "And you have my loyalty, granddaughter. I built Platirius to be the greatest force in the galaxy. My legacy will stand forever. Let us correct everything Revari set in motion when she betrayed us for a Human. Accept my help. Together we'll make things right."

Queen Vivant looked down at his outstretched hand, then into the black fire roaring in his eyes.

P

rincess Tarah watched Princess Teenah spin around the dance floor for the third time and rolled her eyes. King Justin was teaching General Lyric a dance called *Bolero*.

Although she was happy General Lyric would finally receive the happy ending she deserved, she held conflicted feelings about her cousin. He'd nearly succeeded in driving her mother mad. Unlike her sisters, she wasn't ready to forgive and forget so easily.

Unbeknownst to Queen Vivant, she'd snuck to the courtyard and overheard the conversation between her and Gallium. Lately, thoughts of her father had plagued her dreams. If he'd been killed in battle, why was his body still missing? Not a word had been sent to Maieman, his home planet.

Surely King Micah, Queen Marietta, or King Jonah would've found him by now. There were too many unanswered questions surrounding his disappearance. Draining her glass, she stood up to leave.

She'd convince her mother to find out what happened to her father. If foul play were involved, she'd ensure the guilty parties wouldn't receive an ounce of mercy.

A life for a life, she thought.

Queen Vivant firmly secured the palace's doors as she did every night. She knew General Absalom was impeccable at keeping a firm rein on security. Yet, checking the doors had become a part of her routine since the night her father stole her, her sister, and her aunt from Coldarius. It helped to ease her anxiety before she went to bed.

She climbed the stairs to the high balcony just outside her bed chamber. Instead of entering it to prepare for bed, she stood high above Platirius, watching the stars. The moon's brilliant rays shone down on her beautiful face, highlighting the iridescent hues of her eyes, making them shine like diamonds.

Turning to stare off into the distance, her silver eyes slowly turned as black as the night. Clouds formed over the moon, hiding an evil smile settling on her lips.

Join my VIP list

Join my VIP list @ www.dlhannah.com

Author Bio

D.L. Hannah was born in Youngstown, Ohio. She is a writer, entrepreneur, and host of the Amerisogyny podcast. She is a Psi Chi and Alpha Kappa Delta member and earned a Bachelor of Arts degree in Clinical-Community Psychology from Walsh University. For over twenty years, she has been a strong advocate for children diagnosed with Autism. She now lives in North Carolina with her family.

Also by D.L. Hannah

Platirius: Infiltration Book I

Platirius: The Rise of Reve Book II

Platirius: Kikhani vs Platirius Book III

Coldarius: The Origin of Gallium Book I

Coldarius: The Betrayal Book II

JanIus: Pawns Book I

JanIus: Enter the King Book II

JanIus: Platirius vs JanIus Book III

Maieman: Paradox Book I

Maieman: Revelations Book II

www.ingramcontent.com/pod-product-compliance
Lightning Source LLC
Chambersburg PA
CBHW060923180626
46817CB00004B/1377